A
Harlequin
Romance

DEAR PROFESSOR

by

SARA SEALE

HARLEQUIN BOOKS

Toronto • Canada   New York • New York

DEAR PROFESSOR

First published in 1970 by Mills & Boon Limited,
17 - 19 Foley Street, London, England.

Harlequin Canadian edition published September, 1971
Harlequin U.S. edition published December, 1971

Standard Book Number: 373-51524-3.

Copyright, ©, 1970, by Sara Seale. All rights reserved.

Printed in Canada

CHAPTER I

"WHY must you always make the worst of yourself, dear child?" Gilbert Deverell had irritably enquired of his daughter only that morning. It was a remark which had become so habitual with him that Sarah's feelings were seldom hurt, but now in the solitude of the room over the stable which was her own private domain, she remembered and turned to examine her reflection in the discoloured looking-glass that hung on one wall.

She should have been a boy, she thought, inspecting her sharply angled body and coltish limbs with disfavour, then her father might have taken more interest; but he hadn't wanted a son, he had wanted a charming exquisite daughter who flattered his ego and was a constant delight to his eye. If she had possessed only a fraction of Sylvie's looks, she might have found favour, she thought dispassionately, but her mouth seemed too wide and her eyes too big to balance her narrow face; her forehead was too high and those unsightly freckles would be a source of discouragement to anyone.

"There's no getting away from it, I'm just plain homespun," she said aloud, then sat down at the typewriter to compose the last of the letters.

"Dear Professor..." she began as usual, then stopped as Sylvie's voice called to her from the stable yard.

"Hi, Sarah! What are you doing up there?"

"Seconding Father's invitation with a few well chosen words. Come up!" her cousin shouted back. Willie, the mongrel dog, growled with mock savagery at the sound of feet on the outside staircase and took no notice when absently admonished.

"For goodness' sake! Hasn't that animal learnt to

discriminate yet?" Sylvie exclaimed, swinging herself over the threshold where she stood for a moment wrinkling her charming nose fastidiously. "This place stinks like a menagerie! How many more lame ducks have you acquired?"

"No ducks," said Sarah, who was apt to be literal. "Only the same old crow and a couple of rodents — and Willie knows perfectly well who you are. He only growls to keep his end up because you laugh at him. What shall I say to your unexpected suitor?"

Sylvie's face immediately lit up with pleasure and an innocent conceit.

"Do you think he is a suitor?" she said. "I wonder what he's like."

"Don't you remember?"

"Only the beard and a Nose — definitely a Nose!"

Sarah giggled, remembering how they had giggled over the beard, remembering, too, a mischievous Sylvie describing events at that farewell dinner before the departure of some mineralogical commission to the Himalayas. It was never very clear how she herself had become invited except that the party had consisted mostly of students and Sylvie had a habit of collecting enthusiastic young men, but there had been much beer-drinking and juvenile high spirits and the leader of the expedition, who was very much older than the others, had scarcely taken his eyes off Sylvie. Whether or not he really was a professor they never knew, but she, intrigued both by the beard and his silent interest, had started to tease, calling him Professor to his face and inviting flirtation.

"If you should come across a good snow-leopard skin in the Himalayas, Professor, you might remember me," she had said when it was time to say good-bye, and he had replied quite seriously that he would strike a bargain with her. He would certainly oblige to the best of his ability if she, in return, would send him regular news

6

from home. There were no longer, he had said, any relatives left to keep him posted and a year away from civilization could seem a long time without letters.

"So of course I promised," Sylvie had told her amused family. "It's my duty, isn't it, to do what I can to cheer up a pioneer's lonely exile? Besides, a snow-leopard skin would be very nice."

Dear Professor ... How amusing that had seemed at the time ... He had not thought, apparently, to do more than preface his surname with a couple of initials when supplying an address, and when Sylvie had asked what she was to call him, had replied with casual indifference: "Oh, Professor will do."

For the first couple of months Sylvia had kept faith, but then she grew bored. Letter-writing was not her strong suit and she lost interest waiting for the long-delayed replies which seldom contained the kind of complimentary passages she expected. She had in the meantime acquired a fresh admirer who being on the spot and displaying considerable ardour was more to her taste than a chance pen-friend whose claim to her consideration was becoming decidedly tedious. When Sarah, whose imagination was easily captured, had expressed indignant reproaches, Sylvie had retorted carelessly:

"That was all just a silly joke! If you're so concerned with the feelings of a perfect stranger, you'd better take him over yourself. Your typing needs practice more than mine and he'd never know the difference if you just sign your initial. Besides," she had added hurriedly, anticipating the kind of priggish objections that Sarah was apt to raise at times, "as the poor sweet doesn't really know either of us it can't make a hoot of difference to him who supplies the news, and you'll make a much better job of it than me. Look how you enjoy shutting yourself away here and scribbling in that dreary diary no one's allowed to read. You've only got to think of the Professor as a sort of animated journal, and at least those pointless outpourings won't be wasted."

So Sarah, who could appreciate this point, firmly thought of the Professor as a journal and treated him accordingly. The letters took the place of the diary without any perceptible change of intention, but they had afforded her an added pleasure in the knowledge that her thoughts were now shared. She had not realized how much she had built out of a borrowed personality until her father's surprising announcement had shattered her dream-world. What had been make-believe had now become factual and she could have no share in the fruits of her labours. Visitors at Slattery were rare and it was clear from her father's unusual invitation that not only was he impressed by the stranger's correct approach upon the return of the expedition to England, but was convinced that the outcome of this long correspondence could be in no doubt.

As she looked at her cousin, Sarah's thoughts sped back to their childhood; the day she remembered most vividly was the day of Sylvie's arrival and her own excited anticipation. She had been a solitary child, made aware very early of being a disappointment to her father. It was not until Sylvie had come to live with them that she had fully realized that her plainness and lack of grace had been a perpetual affront both to his aesthetic eye and the idealized memory of his dead wife. Having married late in life, and been widowed too early, it was not to be supposed that he would take kindly to the intrusion of the newly orphaned girl of a brother he had not seen for years, and to the child Sarah, arguments between her father and Aunt Fran who had kept house for them had seemed endless and without reason until she had overheard Gilbert observe petulantly that Martin's child would undoubtedly be as plain as his own ugly duckling and that was reason enough for hesitation. Sarah, at eight years old, had not resented the slight on her appearance, being accustomed to frank if unflattering reference to herself, but she had suffered agonies lest her hopes of another child to play with should be dashed.

When the great day had come, however, and she had waited with her father and aunt in the cool, flag-stoned hall to welcome the new arrival, she had known at once that although friendship between the two of them was both desirable and necessary to the smooth running of the household, here was no boon companion to share in her dreams and private gods.

Even at eleven years old Sylvie had been exquisite with her porcelain fairness and fine delicate bones. Sarah had watched with envy the astonished delight in her father's face as he absorbed each facet of this child's astounding beauty and was not at all surprised when he drew her to him, saying softly: "Why, you might have been my own little daughter."

Up in the nursery, Sarah had not known how to offer consolation to the newly bereaved and was very conscious of her own clumsy awkwardness and the three-year gap in their ages which then had seemed to her enormous. She could only offer what was dearest to her and had sacrificed her most cherished possession in the shape of Gloriana, a wooden doll of doubtful pedigree and few visible charms.

"I don't care for dolls. Haven't you got something better than this old thing?" Sylvie had said in her polite, self-possessed little voice, giving Gloriana a push which had sent her flying on to the floor with an ominous sound of breaking joints. Sarah had picked her up, minus two of her wooden limbs, and had great difficulty in remembering that the new cousin was also a guest as rage swelled within her. But it was Sylvie who had burst into tears and was inconsolable until she had been offered another choice more to her liking.

The incident had set the pattern for their future

relationship, for Sylvie had the knack of timely tears, just as she had the less happy knack of rubbing the bloom off things. Gloriana had been painstakingly mended, but Sarah had never cared for her again, just as in later years she had ceased to find pleasure in more adult acquisitions when they did not meet with her cousin's approval. When they quarrelled it was always Sylvie who wept, and since she did it so beautifully with none of the usual facial disfigurement, she generally got her own way.

"You're moaning again. What about that letter you were just about to write to our adopted professor?" Sylvie said, and Sarah giggled.

"It does sound stuffy and middle-aged, doesn't it?" she said.

"He probably is, too, though he isn't a professor at all, of course, but quite an authority in his own field, according to Uncle Gil — lectures and broadcasts and things like that. Uncle Gil, you will have gathered, has been making discreet enquiries, the sly old fox! Here — I'd better do the last letter myself just to show willing," Sylvie said, elbowing her cousin out of the way and sitting down at the typewriter. She ripped out Sarah's sheet from the machine and, inserting another, began again.

"Dear Professor..." As Sarah watched the familiar form of address which she had used for so long being typed out again under Sylvie's careless fingers, a curious feeling of resentment possessed her. There was more of herself in those letters than there was of Sylvie whose ghost she had been, and the solace of communicating with a stranger would be lost to her for ever when he appeared among them in the flesh.

"Supposing he's got the wrong idea?" she said suddenly, and Sylvie giggled.

"If he has, then you must have been leading the poor man up the garden," she said. "*Have* you been indulg-

10

ing in a sort of make-believe romance at second-hand, darling?"

"Of course not! I just rambled on about our daily lives — anything that came into my head that I thought might be of interest."

"How deadly! Just like your diary, in fact. You needn't look so outraged, you idiot — I was only teasing, and you've gone quite pink! You know, Sarah, you wouldn't look bad if you took a little trouble — your freckles hardly show when you blush. Why don't you experiment more with make-up? There's no need, these days, for any girl to put up with the looks the good God gave her."

"I'm not clever with make-up and it wouldn't suit me, anyway," Sarah said a little shortly, and Sylvie shrugged, whipped the sheet of paper out of the machine and signed it with the bold, flamboyant "S" which did duty for her signature and grinned up at her cousin.

"What a good thing you insisted on copying my flourishes when we were at school," she said. "Our deluded professor can never accuse you of forgery since we have the same initials."

"I hope he won't accuse me of anything. Are you getting interested, Sylvie?"

Sylvie looked mischievous.

"I can always be interested in a fresh admirer, even a bearded professor. Besides, he'll do me some good another direction."

Sarah frowned.

"Nick Bannister? I wish you'd finish with him, Sylvie. He's married and there's no future in it. You only want him because he belongs to someone else."

"That's all you know, my dear. I find him attractive and exciting, and I can get him too, if I set my mind to it."

"Even if it means breaking up a home?"

Sylvie's eyes, which really were the authentic colour

11

of violets, immediately filled with reproachful tears.

"That's mean, Sarah. I'm not breaking up anything — he's separated from his wife, as you very well know," she said. "Anyway, I bet she's a bitch."

Sarah smiled reluctantly. There were times when, despite her own inexperience in romantic affairs, she often felt the elder of the two.

"Married men are always misunderstood, so I'm told," she said a little primly, and Sylvie made a face at her.

"So what? It's probably true or they wouldn't be looking around in other directions. Mind your own business, dear prissy cousin, and I'll mind mine," she said, but quite without rancour, and Sarah was silent, knowing herself defeated.

"You'd better address your letter," she said, searching for an unused envelope amongst the litter piled on the table, but Sylvie was already prinking in front of the glass, smiling at her charming reflection with none of the dissatisfaction which Sarah, earlier, had afforded her own.

"Be a love and do it for me. I've got a date in the village," she said carelessly. "Cover up for me if I'm late for the family session before dinner, won't you, darling? Uncle Gil still has old-fashioned ideas about pubs, and married philanderers in particular." She blew a kiss with the airy grace which characterized all her movements, then clattered down the wooden steps outside.

Sarah, from the window, watched her cousin swing over the yard gate and begin picking her way along the moorland track which was the short cut to the village. Sylvie did not really care for the moor with its rough paths and wild expanse of scrub and bracken and heather, but it was simpler to walk to a doubtful rendezvous than to take the car and risk awkward questions. *Cover up for me...* she had said with the careless habit of the years, and Sarah smiled. Hadn't she always covered up, at school, in the holidays; completing essays and other scholastic tasks which had been too much trouble to finish, just as later she had in the same obliging spirit, taken over that impulsive promise to a stranger?

Sarah, hoping that Sylvie would not be late and so upset the evening routine, turned back with pleasure to the little room which was her own escape from family obligations.

Her eyes dwelt lovingly on its roughly plastered walls, the crooked beam which supported the exposed rafters of the high-pitched roof, the floor littered with assorted reminders of her occupation and that of the animals. Here were the treasures of her childhood, salvaged along with the unwanted nursery furniture; favourite books and pictures, dusty rosettes, mementoes of bygone gymkhanas when ponies had been kept for them, and the old school trunk which still housed a miscellaneous collection of forgotten objects which had once been too precious to discard. Here in the company of Willie and any wild creature requiring temporary shelter, she could escape into her own world and daydream undisturbed; here she had taken refuge in her journal and later on found much happiness in writing secret letters to a man she had never met....

She glanced through Sylvie's brief communication, then thrust an envelope into the typewriter and hammered out the name and address with a depressing feeling of finality. When she had sealed up the letter she stood staring down at it with the curious sensation that she had sealed up her private thoughts with it. The stranger with whom she had corresponded was no longer the Dear Professor to whom her journalistic efforts had been addressed, but A. C. Soames Esq., another and quite different stranger. What was he really like, she wondered, remembering the brief con-

13

tents of his replies, and had this proposed visit the significance that was tacitly assumed by the rest of the household? That he desired to further the acquaintance was evident, she thought, pocketing Sylvie's letter, and if he did no more than provide a timely distraction to the undoubted charms of the dashing Mr. Bannister he would have earned his hospitality.

Sarah covered the typewriter, gave the expectant Willie the signature for departure and prepared to take leave of her dumb dependants. There were only three of them now, for it was late September and the lingering echoes of that perfect summer still warmed the days, but when the bad weather came starving birds and the small, weak creatures of the moor would once again need her protection. She fed the animals, rescued part of the neglected journal which was in danger of being torn up by Willie, and ran down the wooden stairway into the yard.

She posted the letter in the box let into one of the pillars of the drive gates with that same sense of finality, and wandered back to the house wishing her unknown correspondent could have remained anonymous. So much of herself had gone into those letters that it was going to be difficult to remember that she had been deputizing for Sylvie, who at this very moment was exerting her charms on somebody else. Unacquainted with the intricacies of an affair, Sarah wondered with mild curiosity what Sylvie and Nick found to talk about during those stolen meetings in the private bar of the village pub, but as she came in sight of the house she forgot about idle speculations in the renewed pleasure of contemplating her home. There was something very satisfying about Slattery, she thought, pausing for a moment to enjoy the brilliant splash of colour of the turning creeper against the grey walls, the little cushions of vivid green the moss made on the slates of the roof, the vine which climbed up and over the porch so thickly that the entrance was always in shadow, and the fiery reflection from the setting sun winking a welcome from the windows. She went briskly round to the back of the house because Willie was not allowed further than the kitchen.

"What's for dinner?" she demanded of Hattie who was presiding over a bubbling cauldron on the range like the witch she very much resembled, but she only stirred the harder and made no reply, it evidently being one of her taciturn days.

"Where's Jed?" Sarah asked, reaching for the bowl of scraps which had been saved for Willie's supper. She was seldom disturbed by Hattie's tacit snubs, for the Cokers, mother and son, had been with them as long as Sarah could remember, and although Hattie's temper was often unpredictable and her tongue sharp, she was part of Slattery and as familiar.

"Down to public most like," she snapped back then, and the cause for her ill-humour seemed clearer. Jed, now a handsome youth of twenty-two, had been promoted some time ago from stable-boy to general handyman, and Hattie who was staunchly chapel had strict views on the evils of drink.

Sylvie, followed by Jed, came into the kitchen at that moment and Hattie turned to eye them both with impartial displeasure.

"Where bin to?" she demanded belligerently of her son, but since he knew she was well aware of the answer he only grinned and made no reply.

"We met at the Fox and Jed walked me home. Why should that make you snappy?" Sylvie said, giving the young man a quick, sidelong glance under her lashes.

"You should know better than to go carousing in the village pub with the hired help."

"What a gorgeous word!" Sylvie exclaimed with a gurgle of laughter. "You make us sound like a couple of debauched fly-by-nights! I do adore you, Hattie, when

15

you go all proper and puritan."

Hattie gave vent to one of her outraged snorts, and Sarah, knowing how her cousin loved to tease, set Willie's dish down on the flagged floor, expecting to hear her relent and explain that she had been meeting a friend and the walk home with Jed was purely accidental, but Sylvie said nothing. She simply went on smiling at the unresponsive young man with slow deliberation and tossed a shining strand of her hair over her shoulder.

"Well, what are you waiting for? You'd best go and brush up too if you don't want to keep your uncle waiting," Hattie snapped. "You'm too old to be hanging around my kitchen making sheep's eyes for a bit of fun."

"Really, Hattie! You don't imagine I have designs on poor Jed, do you?" Sylvie said with mock innocence.

Hattie made no reply and turned back to the stove, but Sarah with greater perception knew that she did. But how absurd, she thought indignantly, and found she had spoken aloud.

"Yes, isn't it?" Sylvie said with cool amusement. "Come on, love, we'd better get busy with our own ablutions, or we'll be late."

"That was mean," Sarah said as they went upstairs together. "You needn't have let Hattie think you'd gone to the pub to meet Jed."

"Well, he didn't deny it, did he? I'm not having Hattie poking her sharp nose into my affairs. I'm old enough to please myself in the matter of my friends."

"Yes, of course," Sarah agreed diplomatically, but she was vaguely uneasy. It was natural, she supposed, that Sylvie should turn a misconception to her advantage since her friendship with Nick Bannister was not approved of, but it seemed unfair to upset Hattie who, for all her sharp tongue, was a loyal servant and had always had a weakness for Sylvie's pretty ways.

"Did you enjoy yourself drinking?" she asked as they

paused at the door of Sylvie's room, and as her cousin bestowed one of her careless embraces upon her she could sense an air of pent-up excitement.

"Dear Sarah, you make it sound like an orgy — just like Hattie!" she said, and the same excitement was in her voice. "I don't patronize our local for the sake of its liquid refreshment, you know. It's just a convenient halfway house for meetings as Nick lives in Tawstock and Uncle Gil's a bit stuffy about having him here."

"Yes, I see," Sarah said, but privately she considered that her usually clever father was not being very subtle. He should know by now that putting obstacles in the way was a sure way of fanning Sylvie's desires.

"Did you post my letter?" Sylvie asked. "Our stuffy professor is going to do me a good turn. Nick got quite heated tonight and *very* possessive. I'm really looking forward to this visit."

"Sylvie —" Sarah began, but she did not finish. She really had no idea what she wanted to say and was only aware of her own increased disturbance, but Sylvie, with one of her rare flashes of intuition, touched her cheek gently and said with soft amusement:

"Darling, you haven't really been working up a kind of make-believe crush for our mutual pen-friend, have you?"

"Of course not!"

"That's good. You're so impressionable, and I wouldn't like you to get hurt."

"Why should I get hurt? I've never met the man, and it was you he thought he was writing to, anyway."

"Yes, of course. I wish I'd vetted some of those letters, though. I wonder if he's kept them."

"Why on earth should he?"

"Well, you kept his."

"Only because I get so few from anyone else."

"But you got a kick out of them, didn't you? Now, don't fly into one of your rages, love, I was only

17

teasing. You saved me hours of dreary homework, so why should I grudge you any fun you may have got out of it? He's probably a dead bore, anyway."

"Probably," Sarah snapped with unaccustomed sharpness, and went into her own room and slammed the door, aware that she had been experiencing the same unexpected rush of childish rage which had possessed her when Sylvie had pushed Gloriana on to the floor so long ago. She had largely outgrown those fits of temper thanks to her father's cool distaste for scenes, and Sylvie's small taunts seldom held real malice. She had intended none now, Sarah knew, already ashamed of her own reactions, and no doubt the Professor, faceless, save for the nebulous distinction of a Beard and a Nose, was indeed a dead bore.

He was to arrive the next day, and early that morning the household arose to an unfamiliar flurry of cleaning and polishing.

"You'd think," shouted Sarah in the throes of bed-making, "that we had royalty coming instead of a dim professor who probably wouldn't notice dust if he saw it."

"They're cherishing Hopes, love," Sylvie shouted back from her own room across the landing. "Uncle Gil may live in a kind of cloud-cuckoo-land where I'm concerned, but he knows he can't divide up your inheritance when he pops off, so — Slattery and your mama's money for you and a respectable husband for me."

"The assumption being that my own chances of a husband are pretty dim."

"Oh, don't be silly! You can be quite attractive in an off-beat kind of fashion when you take any trouble."

"Thanks, but I've no wish to compete in a losing game. All the young men who've ever been to this house

18

took one look at you and fell flat." Sarah spoke with amusement rather than ruefulness and Sylvie crossed the landing and propped herself in the doorway to continue the conversation with greater ease.

"Have you minded?" she asked curiously. Her own conquests had been taken as a matter of course for so long in the household that she had never considered the possibility of Sarah's feelings.

"Not in the least," Sarah replied, thumping her bed into a more respectable shape before covering its lumps with the bedspread. "I suppose a little personal interest might boost one's morale, but I always felt awkward and out of place at those dreadful Saturday night hops in Tawstock you used to drag me to."

"Well," said Sylvie, "you can at least make the best of yourself tonight and not wear just any old thing for dinner. You *are* the daughter of the house, after all, and a guest is entitled to a little extra trouble."

"This particular guest isn't interested in the daughter of the house, so why should I bother? With you around he won't even notice I'm there," Sarah replied, giving her bed a final thump, and Sylvie looked mischievous. It would be rather amusing if the poor sweet really had worked up a kind of imaginary relationship with the Professor and was going to be awkward just to show her indifference, she thought, and said teasingly:

"No reason if you want to be difficult, but I should have thought you'd be thrilled to meet the unknown hero of all those letters."

"Why should I be? I was only filling in for you because you were too lazy to write yourself. I don't even know what he looks like," Sarah said, and went downstairs and out to the stable-room to feed the animals, but she was conscious of a growing reluctance to be confronted with the innocent recipient of her unthinking confidences and was unable to shake off a growing feeling of depression.

At lunch Sylvie said casually:

"You'll have to go into Tawstock and meet the train, Sarah."

"What train?" asked Sarah vaguely.

"The Professor's train, of course, silly. Have you forgotten he's arriving this afternoon?"

"But *you* were going to meet him. You've said all along it was your perks."

"Well, I've changed my mind. I want to set my hair and make myself beautiful. I'm going to make an entrance with a capital 'E' when you have him nicely settled in a and all agog. Uncle Gill approves, don't you, sweetie-pie?"

"Not when you address me in those nauseating terms," her uncle replied, his little white beard quivering with distaste, but his cold eyes twinkled and he appeared to be in a good humour.

"Sorry, darling," Sylvie said with blithe unconcern, and blew him an airy kiss across the table. "Anyway, Aunt Fran thinks it's a good idea to doll myself up nicely for first impressions, don't you, Aunt?"

Frances' eyes rested on her niece a little abstractedly, but she answered quite briskly:

"You always look charming, dear child, but if you want to impress, I can quite understand that a railway platform is hardly a glamorous setting."

"I'm surprised that *you* should adopt that meaningless and overworked word, Frances," her brother rebuked her irritably. "Still, I suppose it's not entirely inappropriate in certain cases, eh, Sylvie?"

Sylvie favoured him with one of her provocative glances under her lashes and smiled without replying, and Sarah became conscious of an unaccustomed and rather horrifying moment of critical appraisal. She saw them both not as the familiar figures who governed her thoughts and affections, but as two strangers speaking lines which meant little to either of them. It was as if the pair of them indulged in a meaningless flirtation and neither one of them cared sufficiently to do more than go through the motions.

"Why are you staring at me like that, dear child? Do you grudge me the natural appreciation of a pretty niece?" Gilbert said with benign rebuke, and she flushed.

"No, of course not. I was thinking of something else," she said quickly, and his eyes focussed on her with closer attention.

"Well, I trust you'll do something about your appearance before going to the station or our guest will think I've sent the stable boy to meet him," he observed with heavy playfulness. He was not, to do him justice, unaware of his parental obligations, but he had never grown out of the habit of treating his daughter as a rather tiresome child.

"I can't go this afternoon. I promised to give them an extra couple of hours at the Home," she said, and only Sylvie recognized the first signs of temper and wished her uncle had a little more tact.

"Nonsense!" he snapped impatiently. "I shall ring them up myself and explain the circumstances. You spend too much time with those unfortunate children as it is, considering you're unpaid."

"Payment has nothing to do with it. The children need me and I like doing it."

"Then if it's simply a question of pleasing yourself you can afford to consider your family's requirements first," Gilbert retorted suavely.

"You don't understand —" she began, her colour mounting. Sylvie said softly: "Don't rise, darling, he's only doing it to tease," and her father went on as if no one had spoken: "I understand perfectly. You are perhaps naturally resenting our guest's reason for a visit, I think, and don't want to play second fiddle. Am I not right, Sylvie?"

"Of course not," Sylvie replied before Sarah could answer. "Sarah couldn't care less about impressing a complete stranger and neither, for the matter of that, do I. So stop picking on the poor sweet. However, my natural vanity is such that I want to make an entrance and focus all eyes, so you *will* meet the train and let me have the field to myself, won't you, Sarah love?"

Sarah's little flutter of rebellion subsided.

"Very well," she said, adding with rather a childish determination to have the last word: "But I shall go as I am and I shall take Willie. The sooner this tiresome stranger gets used to the way I look, the better."

"Pity," her aunt murmured absently, getting up to leave the table. "Still, there's always the evening, and you have a few nice frocks to choose from, dear. Gilbert, have you decided yet on that wine? I rather think that we've kept that Chateau Yquem too long."

CHAPTER II

SARAH was too early for the train and she sat on a platform bench and pondered on the happenings of the morning. It had been ridiculous, she supposed, to oppose such an unimportant decision as to who should meet the train, neither did she understand her own reluctance to oblige except that since posting that last letter she had been aware of an odd sense of loss. It was unfair of the faceless recipient of one's confidences to suddenly put on the solid flesh of a living person, she thought resentfully, then grinned at her own absurdity. It was scarcely the Professor's fault if she had built him into a kind of father-figure, neither could Sylvie be blamed for accepting the situation as it stood. At least no one could take away the innocent pleasure derived from those hours of scribbling in the stable-room and eventually she would go back to the solace of her journal. She wished, all the same, that she was not deputizing for her cousin at the station. It was Friday the thirteenth which seemed ominous and the day had not begun well.

She got to her feet as the train drew into the station and felt suddenly nervous.

"How shall I know him?" she had said to Sylvie before she left the house.

"Just look out for a beard, there can't be many about," Sylvie had replied vaguely, and Sarah scanned the alighting passengers with increasing anxiety. No one appeared to be bearded, and few had the air of travellers expecting to be met. A tall man walking with a limp and a stick passed her without a glance, another, rather older, paused for a moment uncertainly and she opened her mouth to address him, but he was only searching for his ticket and was presently hailed by a tweedy woman who was clearly his wife.

He must have missed the train, Sarah thought, walking slowly back to the barrier, and wasn't sure whether she felt disappointment or relief.

The man with the limp was standing by the bookstall as she came through, idly scanning the paperbacks. There were a couple of much-labelled suitcases beside him and he looked up expectantly as she passed him, then resumed his inspection of the paperbacks. Sarah paused, then she too evinced interest in the bookstall where she could study him surreptitiously out of the tail of her eye. Dark, quite young, and deeply tanned, she observed. His chin was smoothly shaven, but he certainly had a Nose. You were aware of the impressive nature of the nose, Sarah thought, before discovering with something of relief that the deep furrows running from nostril to mouth indicated humour rather than severity, and the slightly unsymmetrical eyebrows gave his face a quizzical look. He glanced up again, aware of her scrutiny, and frowned, and she said the first thing that came into her head.

"The nose and the tan and the foreign labels — it must all add up," she burst out, and one eyebrow rose.

"I beg your pardon?" he said politely, and conscious of how odd her remark must sound to a perfect stranger she moved with the sudden awkwardness so familiar to her family and sent a pile of magazines flying to the ground.

"Oh, goodness!" she exclaimed, feeling herself go crimson as she stooped to retrieve them.

"Allow me," he said with grave courtesy, but she thought she detected an undercuurrent of amusement as he bent to help her, and she found herself wishing, as she observed his well-groomed head at closer quarters, that she had at least found time to run a comb through her tangle of short brown curls.

"Now," the stranger said as he straightened up and

24

brushed the station dust from his well-creased trousers, "perhaps you would care to elucidate?"

"Are you A. P. Soames, Esq.?" she said with a rush, remembering only the more formal means of identification the envelopes had borne. "I mean, are you the Professor?"

He had been looking down at her with rather unnerving deliberation as if he were trying to decide whether she was slightly crazy or just a rather scruffy-looking young woman who was trying to pick him up, but all at once his expression altered and the smile he gave her lent his face an unexpected charm.

"Good heavens, you must be the little cousin — Sarah, isn't it?" he exclaimed. "I'm sorry if I've been unhelpful, but I was expecting Sylvia to meet me."

"And I was expecting a Beard."

"A beard? Oh, I see. I'd allowed mine to grow prior to the expedition. We don't have many facilities for our early morning ablutions on some of these trips. Is your cousin not here?"

"No, she isn't. She wants to make an Entrance, so she's dolling herself up in advance. Can you manage your luggage? There are never any porters here when you want them and if you ring the bell they'll let you wait all night. The car's outside."

His lips twitched and she knew she had been talking like the gauche child he must take her for, but the unexpectedness of his total disparity to the Professor of her imaginings had thrown her off balance.

"You're very forthright, aren't you? From what I remember of her, your cousin would scarcely need to refresh the memory with additional aids," he remarked, and picked up one of the cases.

"Well, you certainly *talk* like a professor!" she retorted, and immediately felt horrified at such rudeness. He could hardly be blamed for making it clear that his interest lay elsewhere, for that was to be expected,

25

but she was experiencing a most irrational sense of being cheated since it was she who had kept that memory green.

"Do I? Well, I don't aspire to such a learned rank, you know. That was just your cousin's idea of a joke. If you show me where your car is, I'll dump this and come back for the others."

Her resentment vanished as he made for the door, leaning on his stick to balance the heavy suitcase in the other hand. She had forgotten he was lame and she immediately forgave him for disappointing her in the more familiar emotion that any afflicted creature could arouse in her. She seized the second suitcase, dragging it after him, and when he turned to protest, said breathlessly:

"You never said you were lame."

"It's nothing permanent. I broke a bone in my ankle not long before we sailed for home, and it's taken rather a time mending," he replied. "Is this your car?"

A. P. Soames, Esq. deposited the cases in the boot, glanced a shade quizzically at Sarah already seated behind the wheel as if he doubted her ability to drive, then climbed meekly in beside her.

"You needn't be nervous, I've passed my test," she informed him coldly, trying to clear the windscreen which had become completely fogged with Willie's breath, adding as she saw him stretch out an inviting hand: "You'd better not take liberties with Willie till he knows you. He doesn't like strangers." Willie, however, with the incalculable perversity of animals, let her down. He placed two muddy paws on the stranger's well-tailored shoulders and swept a long, wet tongue from ear to chin.

"Should I take that as a royal mark of favour or will he bite me if I'm too familiar in return?" the guest enquired mildly, wiping his face with a spotless handkerchief.

26

"It means he's accepted you, which is very surprising," Sarah replied still more coldly. She would have a bone to pick with Willie when they got home.

"Is it? But I like animals."

"Do you?" This at least was in his favour. "Well, that's just as well. I have a sort of animal sanctuary in the stable-room and you can be useful and feed them if I'm not around." It was quite absurd and not very dignified to indulge in schoolgirl repartee just because he was not what she had expected and had laughed at Willie, and she started the car and drove out of the station yard with a flourish, thinking the sooner she could hand him over to Sylvie the better.

"I seem to have got off on the wrong foot," he observed mildly when the town was left behind and Sarah had taken the moorland road back to Peavey village.

"Well, you weren't what I expected," she replied, but she was already regretting her unaccustomed ill-humour. She wanted to point out her favourite landmarks on the way home and to share her delight in the splendour of the moor.

"Don't take against me before you even know me, Sarah. I may need the little cousin's support."

Well, that seemed plain enough, thought Sarah, and replied with cool directness: "I've never had any influence with my cousin, if that's what you mean. She's always known what she wants and manages to get it. Have you fallen for her — seriously, I mean?"

He laughed.

"Now you're being too curious — or perhaps you're just adolescent and romantic. Love at first sight is strictly for the very young, you know."

"I'm not an adolescent. I'm eighteen, and I'm not at all romantic," Sarah said, and he gave her a quick glance. No, she was not an adolescent, despite appearances, he thought, neither did she display the usual youthful imagination but simply stated a fact.

27

"You must forgive me again. Eighteen sounds young to me, but these days girls seem to become young women when they're barely out of the schoolroom."

"It depends on how you've been reared," she replied quite seriously. "Sylvie's three years older than me, but you'll find she is much the younger."

"Will I, indeed? What an extraordinary girl you are. Weren't you brought up together?"

"Oh, yes — at least since Sylvie was eleven, but you must have realized yourself when you met her that she's always been admired and cherished and made much of."

"And you haven't?"

"Oh, no, don't misunderstand me. Sylvie's different and rather special. I only meant that too much spoiling can stop you from growing up. There's no time, you see, to make a world of your own, no point in coming to terms with yourself when everything's there for the asking."

She had spoken unthinkingly, clarifying her mind as she used to when writing the letters, but she had been too unguarded.

"And yet, you know, your cousin expressed much the same views when she wrote. Perhaps the two of you are closer than you realize."

"Perhaps we are," she said shortly, wishing she had held her tongue. Far from making her point clear she had doubtless merely convinced him that she resented her cousin's superior attractions.

They were home before she had the time to interest him in the countryside and, annoyed with herself for missing her opportunity by being led into personalities, she ushered A. C. Soames, Esq. into the house with polite formality, made the necessary introductions with all speed and then took herself off to the stable-room. Sylvie had been nowhere in evidence and was probably still upstairs fixing her hair. She would, thought Sarah, undoubtedly make her grand entrance before dinner and

28

it was going to be interesting to see how she reacted to this chance acquaintance who was neither bearded, middle-aged or dull.

Afterwards, Sarah recalled the evening with mixed feelings.

Sylvie's much-vaunted entrance had fallen a little flat since Gilbert had chosen that moment to invite the guest to admire the contents of a cabinet and she was obliged to present her charming pose to the discouraging unawareness of a pair of masculine backs.

Sarah's sympathies were immediately aroused. She thought Sylvia was looking exquisite in a cloudy creation that was new to her and her sense of occasion was outraged by such bad stage-management on the part of her family.

"Father! Sylvie would like a glass of sherry," she said in a clear, accusing voice, and the two men turned at once.

"Ah!" said Gilbert with rather forced bonhomie. "And now you can see the gem of my collection, my dear fellow — a perfect piece of Dresden, m'mm? Is she as exquisite as you remember her?"

Sarah felt the familiar little twinge of embarrassment that her father's more fulsome remarks could still evoke, but the guest had no such reservations. His eyes travelled over Sylvie with slow deliberation, then he smiled, that warm, humorous smile which Sarah had unexpectedly found so attractive.

"Yes, indeed," he said gravely. "How do you do, again, Miss Sylvie Deverell?"

It wasn't fair, thought Sarah, suddenly angry, that her adopted pen-friend should turn out like this, and she watched her cousin curiously for a sign that she too was taken by surprise. But whatever Sylvie may have been thinking, she was too well prepared to give herself away. She merely smiled politely and shook hands, then deliberately turned her attention to her uncle, teasing him, offering him naive openings for a further airing of his views, and looking quite lovely in the flattering lamplight.

It was altogether a very pretty performance, Sarah thought appreciatively, wondering how one acquired such skill with so little opportunity for practising it. Aunt Fran chose that moment to enquire kindly why her younger niece had not put on a more becoming dress, which focussed unwelcome attention upon Sarah and caused her father to observe with heavy pleasantry:

"Alas, my ugly duckling has no desire to turn into a swan, but that need hardly trouble us on this occasion, m'mm? By the same token, Sylvie, you are neglecting your duties. Isn't it time you stopped flattering your old uncle and exerted your charms in another quarter?"

Sylvie got up at once, refilled her empty glass on the way, then sat down beside the guest.

"Did you remember my snow-leopard?" she asked, her head on one side.

"Oh, yes," he replied with lazy amusement, "but I found you something more suitable."

"Oh! That sounds rather stuffy. What is it?" she said, looking disappointed.

"Never you mind. You must wait till I've unpacked, and I don't think you'll find my side of the bargain stuffy."

"The bargain?"

"Had you forgotten you held me to ransom? In that case those letters were certainly an act of grace."

"Oh, the letters," Sylvie said airily, adding quickly: "You know I'd never have recognized you without that beard. You don't look like a professor at all now. What are we to call you? Mr. Soames sounds rather formal after all this time and we can't go on addressing you as Dear Professor."

"My name's Adam," he said, watching her with

30

appreciation, and Gilbert rose as Hattie sounded the gong for dinner saying approvingly:

"A good name that. Earthy, significant. Adam, the first of the human race. Do you not think, my dear fellow, that our Sylvie would have made an exquisite Eve?"

"Oh, really, Uncle Gil!" Sylvie exclaimed, forgetting her role of sophistication in a more natural moment of embarrassment.

"Your uncle is right, you know," Adam said, also rising. "But don't let that disturb you. There are more ways than one of disposing of that apple."

She looked up at him with widening eyes, but if she had read anything significant into that remark, his smile was merely the polite smile of a guest who knows he is expected to turn a suitable compliment. As they went in to dinner Sylvie noticed his limp for the first time and exclaimed with charming impudence: "Oh, you're a lame duck! Sarah *will* be pleased — she collects them."

"Now, pussy-cat, you mustn't tease. It's not polite to draw attention to infirmities," her uncle said indulgently, and Sarah felt uncomfortable. To pay the guest out for the look of amused enquiry he sent her, she enquired with mock solicitude whether he would care for a footstool under the table and, her offer politely refused, they all sat down to dinner.

For most of the meal the conversation was divided between the two men. Adam talked well and Gilbert who, when he was sufficiently interested to forget his self-absorption, could prove an attentive host, was plainly taken with his guest. If nothing else, thought Sarah, her discomfort forgotten, as she listened with eagerness to accounts of his Himalayan experiences, this visit would distract her father from trivialities. It could be, she reflected reasonably, that a wholly feminine household might contribute very largely to masculine bouts of intolerance. But Sylvie looked sulky. She had

31

expected to be the centre of attraction, dividing her favours between the two men while she established contact more with the stranger who appeared to have distinct possibilities. It was too bad of Uncle Gil to monopolize him like this, and Sarah's rapt attention to accounts of boring discoveries in outlandish parts of the globe was frankly irritating.

Only at the end of the evening was Sylvie restored to her first sense of pleasure in the guest's arrival. Sarah was in the kitchen giving Hattie a hand with the washing-up and Aunt Fran had successfully captured her brother's attention over some domestic matter she wished to discuss. Sylvie, aware for some time that the guest's eyes had been resting on her with encouraging awareness, sat down beside him and said with the coaxing air of a little girl who had waited long enough for a promised treat:

"Mayn't I see my present now, please? It's been an awfully boring evening with all this technical talk, and I do so want to get to know you."

He looked down at the exquisite face upturned to his, reflecting that it was something of a miracle that memory hadn't played him false as could so often happen. She was just as fresh and lovely as she had seemed that night of his departure and it was remarkable that despite the flippancies of that occasion she had been serious enough to abide by her promise.

"Don't you feel you know me any better after all those obliging chronicles?" he asked, and she looked vague for a moment.

"Oh, those!" she said. "You didn't reply very promptly."

"No, I suppose I didn't, but we were so often out of reach of civilized communications, and there was never much time for settling down to leisurely epistles. Were you disappointed?"

"No," she answered with truth, since his spasmodic

replies to Sarah's outpourings had long since ceased to interest her.

"Well," he said, "we can always begin again, but I've learnt quite a lot about you, all the same."

"Have you?" she said, wondering what Sarah could have found to say that could have been of any possible interest. "Then please may I know what you found for me that you considered more suitable than a gorgeous snow-leopard?"

"Very well," he said, "I'll go and fetch it."

He had brought her a kaftan which he said he had been given to understand was all the rage at the moment, and this at least was the genuine article and no ready-made western copy. It was a lovely piece of work and the hand-embroidered material was exquisite. Gilbert's collector's instinct was immediately aroused and it was he who insisted that Sylvie should put the robe on and give them a fashion show.

When she had gone upstairs to change, he cocked an enquiring eyebrow at his guest and said with delicate suggestive delicateness:

"In my young day, my dear fellow, a gift of that sort would have had a definite significance, but I don't suppose you had any more serious thought than pairing beauty with beauty, m'mm?"

Sarah came back into the room as her father was speaking and stood for an awkward moment in the doorway waiting for the guest's reply. Whether or not Adam Soames was aware that the remark could be construed as a somewhat premature enquiry as to his intentions, he gave nothing away but smiled absently.

"Well, it struck me as a more fitting piece of adornment than a leopard skin, certainly. Your niece is hardly the type for exotic furs, wouldn't you say?" he said, and Gilbert rather hastily agreed.

"Of course, of course — much too delicate and exquisite for the trappings of a *femme fatale*," he said, and turned with relief as his niece reappeared, this time making an entrance which no one ignored.

"Perfect!" her uncle exclaimed delightedly. "Quite perfect, my dear. Wasn't that a brilliant choice for a man who had only one meeting on which to base his judgement, Sarah?"

Sarah would have liked to find the right words in which to express her admiration, for she thought both her cousin and the exquisite garment had a fairy-tale beauty that was quite breathtaking, but she was too uncomfortably aware of the complacent satisfaction underlying her father's extravagances, of her aunt's sudden air of withdrawal and the faint suggestion of cynical appreciation in Adam Soames' silence to do more than stammer a few inadequate phrases.

Gilbert gave a little shrug and said coldly:

"Not very generous, are you? If you took a little more trouble with your own appearance there would be no need to grudge your cousin a word of praise."

"Now, Uncle, that's very unkind," said Sylvie quickly. "Sarah's the first to say nice things, as you should know, and it would only be natural if she's a wee bit envious of such a lovely thing as this. You shall try it on, darling, when we go to bed, and preen to your heart's content in front of every mirror."

"Thanks, but I could never do justice to a garment like that. If you'll all excuse me, I'm going down to the stable-room for a last look at the animals, so I'll say good-night. It's getting late," Sarah said, and spoke more ungraciously than she intended because her cousin's rare moments of championship always touched her. It was no surprise to hear her father remark as she closed the door:

"I hope you'll make allowances for my gauche daughter while you're with us, Soames. The poor child is rather overshadowed, as you must have seen for yourself, and the few eligible young men in these parts lose

34

their hearts elsewhere, alas!"

He had gestured complacently towards his niece as he spoke, and Sarah slammed out of the house, consumed with the old childish fury. It was monstrous of her father to point out her lack of appeal to a perfect stranger! She had not cared in the past when a tentative admirer had, upon meeting Sylvie, immediately transferred his attentions, for she had never been sufficiently interested, but she had a personal stake in the Professor, and she was not prepared to be humoured or perhaps even pitied by a stranger who unwittingly knew more about her than he was aware of.

For the next few days Slattery seemed to wear a novel air of unfamiliarity at the unusual advent of a visitor, but by the end of the week the guest had ceased to be a stranger. It was rather odd, thought Sarah, how quickly Adam Soames had seemed to settle among them. He was, she supposed grudgingly, one of those adaptable individuals one read about who could fit themselves into any environment and become the perfect guest. If he was making himself agreeable to pave the way for more serious intentions, he was succeeding very well, she thought, aware that the whole household had relaxed in a pleasurable state of anticipation, but whatever the case, he seemed in no hurry to sweep the expectant Sylvie off her feet. Perhaps he was just being clever, Sarah thought, observing with interest her cousin's practised little flights of coquetry which seemed to provoke amusement rather than provocation, but every so often she caught an expression in his eyes which had become very familiar in the glances of other admirers.

Sylvie herself seemed puzzled and frankly disappointed by his failure to conform to the usual pattern.

"Well, you can hardly expect him to press you to his manly bosom after only a week!" Sarah protested during one of their late-night sessions in Sylvie's bedroom.

"Why not? The others do," Sylvie countered

35

impatiently. "If it was love at first sight and all that, he's had a whole year to simmer."

"I don't think he believes in love at first sight. He said it was strictly for adolescents."

"When did he say that?"

"When I drove him back from Tawstock. I'd asked him, by way of making conversation, if he'd fallen for you seriously."

"Really, Sarah! What a thing to blurt out on first acquaintance!" Sylvie exclaimed with shrill annoyance. "No wonder he thinks you're a bit touched. Why can't you keep your mouth shut?"

"Did he say that?" It was not very kind, Sarah reflected, considering she had done her best to cheer up his exile, but of course he wasn't to know that, and she was fully aware that, just as her limbs often betrayed her into clumsiness, so did her unguarded tongue.

"Well, not exactly," Sylvie conceded grudgingly, "but he thinks you're odd. You haven't made much effort to be pleasant to him, have you?"

"I don't think I'm rude. I just keep out of his way and mind my own business. It's you he's interested in, so why should you care if I don't fall over myself to please?"

"I don't, but he not unnaturally thinks you don't like him. It could, of course, be the other way on, though, couldn't it, darling? You did work up rather a thing over those letters and he hasn't turned out stuffy after all. Do you find him attractive?"

"I've never thought about it," Sarah replied somewhat tartly, aware that if not strictly true, it was probably the safest answer to make.

"Oh, well," said Sylvie, whose ill-humour never lasted for long, "it doesn't really matter, does it? But you might take a little more trouble with yourself in the evenings. It's no fun for me to grab all the male attention for lack of any competition."

Sarah went away laughing. Sylvie could be just as naive as herself when she forgot her little sophisticated poses and Sarah supposed that even the acknowledged beauties of this world might find it dull if conquests were too easily come by. So she obligingly took pains with her appearance the next evening and was quite surprised to observe what a little care and the flattery of lamplight could do for her. She could never be called pretty, she thought, regarding herself in the looking-glass with a critical eye, but she might have other qualities. The old brown dress had seen better days, but its lines were good and were kind to her sharp bones. Her summer tan was beginning to fade, she noticed regretfully, and those hated freckles would soon be exposed as the blemishes they were, but tonight they seemed no more than a powdering of gold which was not displeasing and her hair, the one item of her appearance that gave her satisfaction because it was no trouble, curled closely about her head, lending her a boyish charm.

She went downstairs, a little shy of facing her family and hoping that her father would forbear to comment, but it was Sylvie who, probably with the best of intentions, focussed all eyes upon her.

"Darling, you're positively glam! Just see what you can do when you try!" she exclaimed. "Doesn't she look nice, Uncle Gil? Adam, isn't she attractive when she takes trouble?"

Sarah stood there awkwardly, knowing she had gone scarlet. She could have hit her cousin for whose sake she had made the effort and, conscious of Adam's eye upon her with grave deliberation, she had a dreadful suspicion that he would imagine he was the cause. He only smiled, however, and murmured to Sarah with a twinkle:

"One's family can be rather obtuse at times, can't they? Don't let it throw you."

"Throw me?"

"Send you off balance. There has to be a first time for everything."

"I don't know what you mean. I only took a bit more trouble tonight because Sylvie said it was dull having no competition." She had only meant to disabuse him of any mistaken ideas he might have been harbouring thanks to her father's tactlessness, but she realized too late that such a remark might well be equally misconstrued and felt herself colouring again.

He observed her thoughtfully as if deliberating on his next observation, then asked quite mildly:

"Why do I bring out your prickles?"

"You don't really," she answered rather hastily. "Sometimes I have a lot on my mind."

"Have you, indeed? Well, that explains it, of course. I was afraid you had taken a dislike to me."

She looked at him with mute appeal, her high forehead creasing in the worried lines which her aunt deplored.

"Oh, no," she said then. "Oh, no, dear Professor, how could I possibly?" She thought he gave her rather a curious look but was unaware of having spoken at all strangely. She only knew that despite her instinctive withdrawal, he might not be, after all, so very far removed from the imagined recipient of her confidences, and the discovery disturbed her.

"Well, that's very pleasant hearing," he said with a certain briskness, and she wondered whether he had caught some unwelcome undercurrent in her reply and was regretting his kindly efforts to put her at ease.

"In any case, it's hardly sensible to rush to conclusions at such short acquaintance, is it?" she said with deliberate coolness.

"Very true," he replied. "Well, I'm glad to be proved wrong. You see, I feel I know you all so well, thanks to Sylvie's flair for description. This pleasant room with its

38

muted colours and old period pieces was exactly what I expected, down to the copper urn for flowers which always stands on the tallboy by the door... it was almost like revisiting one's old home to walk into your stone-flagged hall and know where each door led to... even Hattie was familiar and perfectly recognizable as a benevolent witch... only you, for some reason, never quite come into focus. Don't you two get on?"

She had listened, fascinated, to this reconstruction of the information she herself had supplied and since forgotten, understanding now why he had been able to fit into their family life so effortlessly, but it would be necessary to remember in future that she must remain ignorant of matters which purported to arise out of someone else's private correspondence.

"Of course we get on," she answered shortly. "She probably thought you wouldn't be very interested."

He raised one eybrow as if he detected resentment in her reply and said pleasantly:

"But naturally I'm interested. Sylvie's cousin is, after all, more important than Hattie and Jed and most of the inhabitants of Peavey village whose sayings and doings I must know by heart. I must get to know you better, Sarah."

But he knew all about her, she thought with a shock of surprise, remembering how much of herself had gone into those letters, but as she remembered, too, how easy it had become to forget she was voicing her own opinions and not Sylvie's, she experienced her first doubts. She was about to reply with polite reciprocation in the matter of better acquaintance, but his eyes had already wandered to Sylvie with a hint of impatience as if he had been waiting to catch her attention, and Sarah moved away quickly, ashamed of the eagerness with which she had found herself responding to a casual moment of interest.

CHAPTER III

THE days passed tranquilly enough and it seemed safe to assume that Adam's courtship was no longer in doubt. He and Sylvie would go off together on nameless expeditions with Sylvie driving the family car and doing the honours of the countryside with charming enthusiasm. But like most of her enthusiasms the novelty soon wore off, and she would return at the end of a day bored with her escort's professional interest in the mineralogical curiosities to be found on the moor and not a little piqued by his slowness in availing himself of proffered opportunities.

"He's more interested in grubbing up bits of rock and fossil than having a cosy petting party and getting things going," she complained to Sarah. "Nick could certainly give him a pointer or two when it comes to a spot of smooching."

"He doesn't strike me as that sort of person," Sarah replied, mildly astonished, as she so often was, by her cousin's view of romance. "If a man has serious intentions, I imagine he would take things slowly, feeling his way."

"Well, he could feel his way a sight more actively as far as I'm concerned," Sylvie retorted crossly. "He hasn't even kissed me yet!" She spoke so much like a spoilt little girl cheated out of her rightful due that Sarah laughed.

"Well, it's early days and I don't expect he'd get much opportunity for practising gentle dalliance stuck in the middle of nowhere for months on end," she said, and found that the Professor's failure to behave in the expected manner pleased her inordinately.

"Yes, I suppose. Well, I'll have to ginger him up with a little hot-blooded competition. Nick's complaining

40

that I neglect him, and I certainly miss his far more satisfactory attentions."

"Sylvie, be careful," Sarah said without pausing to choose her words. "This may all be a game to you, and Nick is perfectly capable of playing it his way, but it's not fair to egg the Professor on if all you want is a bit of excitement."

"Oh, well..." Sylvie said, brightening visibly as she heard Adam's voice calling to her from the garden, "I expect if I'm honest, I'm just a wee bit disappointed after all the family build-up on account of those stupid letters. I wonder what our dear Professor would say if he knew the horrid truth. Be seeing you!"

She vanished through the french windows all smiles again and Sarah was left with the same uneasy reflection. A. C. Soames, Esq., she thought, was not at all the sort of person to take kindly to practical jokes, and the fact that no joke was intended would scarcely make much difference. She wondered if Sylvie would confess to the deception when and if the Professor finally proposed, and whether he would remember enough of the letters' contents to trip her up if she didn't...

For the next few days Sylvie put her plans into practice. She treated Adam to a certain evasive coolness, though careful to wear her prettiest dresses to catch the eye, and had an undisclosed prior engagement when he suggested taking her out. As usual Sarah observed these tactics with the respect that her cousin's skill in these matters always roused in her, but she had an uneasy feeling that the Professor, for all his disparaged potentials, saw through these charming subterfuges and was not a whit disturbed.

One evening, Sylvie suggested that all three of them should visit the Running Fox as an excuse for a walk to the village which would not be too far for Adam's weak ankle.

"Our local is rather a show piece and it would be nice

for Sarah to have a break. Doll yourself up a bit, love, and let's give the village lads a treat," she said.

Sarah assumed, since she was to be included in the party, that Sylvie already had a date with Nick Bannister and intended making a foursome to pair her off with Adam while she flirted provocatively with Nick. Sylvie, who read a great many romantic novels, was, she knew, a firm believer in playing off one man against another in order to create interest, but it seemed, once introductions had been made and they were settled in a corner of the bar parlour with their drinks, that it was Nick who was out of favour. Adam received all the smiles and attention and Nick was left to reward Sarah's uninspired efforts at conversation with none too good a grace. She supposed they had quarrelled again, and Adam was evidently being used to some purpose, judging by the growing signs of temper in the young man's good-looking face. By the way he glowered across at Adam, it seemed plain that Sylvie must have made a good story out of the faithful pen-friend turning up romantically as a prospective suitor, she thought, but observing the look of amusement on Adam's face as he responded gallantly if a trifle absently to her cousin's charming overtures, Sarah suspected that he was quite aware of her tactics.

"What car are you running now?" she asked Nick, trying to find some subject that would interest him. She had never been good at small talk, having had little practice in the social exchanges which came so naturally to Sylvie, but as he was concerned very lucratively with the motor trade it seemed a safe opening. He replied with a salesman-like string of technical details advertising the excellence of his latest sports model which left her ignorant but politely attentive, then evidently deciding to take a leaf out of Sylvie's book, changed his manner and deliberately set out to charm her.

She sat listening to his practised little pleasantries with

a curiosity mixed with a desire to laugh. She was under no illusion that he found her in any way attractive, but she had to admit that he could make himself very convincing. Perhaps it was not so surprising that Sylvie found him exciting, with his sleek blond looks and those very blue eyes that could signal such bold messages of sexual awareness.

Her own reactions could hardly be described as encouraging, but she did her best and very soon Sylvie's attention began to wander and she looked with disfavour and some surprise at the plain little cousin who seemed to be stealing her thunder. Sarah gave her a surreptitious wink at one point which met with no answering acknowledgment, and when Adam got up to order another round of drinks she slid over to the seat next to Nick.

"You mustn't turn poor Sarah's head with your nice line in seduction, darling," she said with a little proprietorial air. "She isn't used to young men who can make pretty speeches without meaning a word of it."

"And what about your Professor? Is he used to being worked on just as a convenience?" he retorted with a hint of renewed temper, but his eyes ran over her with the unspoken assurance that he found her desirable and she moved a little closer to him.

"I wouldn't know," she said demurely. "Anyway, he's rather dull."

Adam came back with the drinks and finding Sylvie's chair vacant, sat down beside Sarah.

"What do you think of our funny little local?" she asked, hoping he wasn't hurt by Sylvie's sudden desertion and resenting the fact that she had called him dull.

"Very pleasant," he replied a little absently. She smiled, satisfied that whatever he privately thought, he seemed unconcerned by a change of partners, and felt no need to do any more in the matter of polite conversation.

Adam, relieved that she appeared to be an undemanding companion who did not expect to be entertained with small talk, sat looking about him with an unexpected little twist of nostalgia. In just such small inns off the beaten track had he and Meg met in the days of their leisurely courtship and explored each other's minds and dreamed their dreams by open hearths sweet with the scent of burning applewood ....

"What were you thinking?" Sarah asked him softly, and he answered with the same awareness of something shared which he had felt with Meg:

"Of the evocative power of certain scents. Wood smoke is particularly nostalgic — and burning peat."

"Yes," she said, sniffing the smoke-laden air appreciatively, and wondering what sort of memories it had stirred in him. She felt very content sitting beside him in companionable silence, listening to the clink of glasses and the friendly murmur of voices coming from the public bar next door. She had quite forgotten the other two until Sylvie burst into a peal of delighted laughter at some whispered sally, and Nick, completely restored to his usual bonhomie, got up to fetch another round of drinks.

Sarah refused, and Adam, catching her eye with a decided twinkle, suggested that the two of them should leave now since it would take him longer to walk home with his gammy leg.

"Bannister will doubtless see you back when you're ready to go," he said, getting up from the table, and Sylvie, plainly accepting his departure as a sign that the withdrawal of her interest had upset him, smiled at him with mischievous comprehension and sped him on his way.

"Don't trouble about me, Professor," she said with the old impudence. "Jed's in the public bar and he's used to walking me home when Nick can't oblige."

It was growing dark as they came out of the Fox and

Sarah stood for a moment gulping down the freshness of the evening air and counting the lights which were appearing one by one in the cottage windows.

She became aware that Adam was waiting patiently, leaning on his stick, and knew that she had been mooning again.

"Did you want to stay?" he asked, evidently misinterpreting her tardiness in starting for home, then added a little wryly, as she turned to walk beside him: "I thought, since we were obviously intended to entertain one another for the rest of the evening, we would enjoy ourselves better out of doors. It was getting a bit stuffy in there."

"Yes, it was, wasn't it?" she said, wondering if, after all, he had minded. "Sylvie's rather like a child in some respects, you know. She loves playing games."

"That, of course, is self-evident, but it's not always very wise," he replied, and she glanced up at him quickly.

"I'm sorry if you were upset," she said shyly, and his sudden laughter took her by surprise.

"Dear Sarah, how naive you are," he said, but there was no ridicule in his amusement. "I'm much too old and disillusioned to be caught by such obvious manoeuvres. It was the other chap I was thinking of."

"Nick? I should have thought he was well able to take care of himself. Anyway, he's married."

"Which doesn't greatly signify these days. I wasn't, as it happens, concerned for his possible feelings. He just struck me as a type it would be wiser not to play games with. Have you known him long?"

"Not very long. He rented a flat in Tawstock a few months ago when his firm took over from Banks. It's Bannisters now, of course, and very smart and up to date."

"Young Bannister strikes me as a smart young man so doubtless his business will prosper. I must get him to look out for a reliable second-hand car for me. I sold my old one before we left for the Himalayas and I will need something when I start work again."

"Yes, you do that. It will please Sylvie," Sarah said rather idiotically, and was not surprised when he replied somewhat dryly that he was more concerned with pleasing himself.

His pace was beginning to slacken as the hill grew steeper and she said:

"Do take my arm up to the top. Devon hills can be horribly tough."

He smiled, but did not remind her that he was accustomed to very much rougher going than this, and obligingly slipped a hand through the crook of her elbow. Arm in arm they followed the courting couples up the hill, and Sarah felt suddenly absurdly happy. When they reached the top she insisted that he rested before starting on the short cut back across the moor, and they sat in a springy patch of heather while she pointed out familiar landmarks.

"That's Ramstor over on the skyline — a pair of eagles once nested there ... and that group of rocks where the ponies are sheltering is Chuff Tor ... and if it wasn't getting dark you would see the stone crosses that mark the old monks' way where the coffins used to be carried across the moor before there were roads ... there's a piskie pool at the bottom of Chuff Hollow where you throw in coins, and if they've disappeared the next time you come it means your wish will come true."

"A piskie pool?"

"Pixie to you, but we call them piskies in these parts. I'll take you there one day if you like, and Granny Coker who lives there in an ancient caravan will tell your fortune as well."

"A double insurance against ill-luck, so to speak. Yes, I know about Granny. Are you superstitious, Sarah?"

"A little. You can't live cheek by jowl with the moor without coming across queer things. The disappearing

46

coins, of course, are just Granny's perks, though you pretend to believe the piskies take them. If she likes you, she swipes them after you've gone just to encourage you to throw in more next time."

Adam laughed.

"A shrewd old lady by all accounts. Is she a relation of your Hattie?"

"Hattie doesn't own to her, having been born a Smale with as strong views on gypsies and fortune-tellers as she has on drink, but Jed likes to boast a bit as do most of the Cokers here about. It's a kind of status symbol to have a witch in the family, you see."

"What a novel variation on keeping up with the Joneses! I confess I find myself bewildered by the recurrence of names over the village shops."

"Yes, names can be very confusing in these parts. Peavey abounds with Cokers and Smales and Dingles, and I suppose once they were all related. Are you rested now, Adam? I think we ought to make a move because Father will be upset if we do him out of his nightly ritual with the sherry."

She got up as she spoke and held out a solicitous hand to help him. He took it gravely, but there was a hint of laughter in his voice as he said:

"How very charming you can be when you forget your prickles, or is it just that I qualify as a lame duck?"

It was nearly dark now. A little breeze had got up and blew between them carrying the moorland scents of thyme and gorse and peat which was so familiar to her, and she looked up at him eagerly, wondering if she imagined a hint of tenderness in his eyes. His hand still rested in hers and she became very much aware of the warm pressure of his fingers and her own unbidden desire to turn her foolish day-dreams into reality.

"We say prackles in these parts, and I don't think you really qualify as a lame duck, Professor," she replied

47

rather primly, and he released her hand and stooped to pick up his stick.

Sarah watched Adam and Sylvie set out the next day, aware of a change of intention in Adam, and she experienced a rueful admiration for Sylvie's tactics. How easy it must be, she thought, to get what you wanted when blessed with such extravagant endowments. It did not occur to her that Adam Soames, thirty-ish and much travelled, was far too experienced to be taken in by feminine tricks unless he wished it; she only hoped that Sylvie would be kind and reward him with gentleness. She found herself wondering as she pedalled to the village how Adam would propose. Would he look down at Sylvie with that tenderness she had glimpsed in his eyes last night, and would Sylvie, too, experience that sudden desire to warm herself at another's fire?

Sylvie, though she felt none of these things, had no cause to think the day wasted. They had driven at her suggestion to Torquay for lunch and a look at the shops. The sophisticated plushiness of that fashionable resort's most expensive hotel was not Adam's idea for promoting courtship, but Sylvie, who was attired in her most elegant outfit, had clearly expected to be shown off with pride and extravagance, and indeed she graced her opulent surroundings so well and was so naively delighted with the admiring attentions she attracted that Adam began to enjoy himself.

"You're like a child snatching at anything bright and colourful. You really enjoy all this fuss and attention, don't you?" he said as they waited for their coffee.

"Well, I don't get much opportunity to show myself off," she replied with charming candour. "Pretty clothes and a pretty face are wasted stuck away on the moor, and Uncle Gil never goes anywhere."

"And yet, you know, I didn't get the impression that you hankered after the fleshpots from your letters."

48

She looked down at her plate, then quickly up again through her lashes.

"Didn't you?" she said vaguely. "Well, I can't remember now what I wrote about."

"Very likely not, but you showed, I think, quite a different side of yourself."

"How?" She would sooner have changed the subject which might prove dangerous, but she was intensely curious about anything concerning herself.

"Possibly the real you came through — the Sylvie who is concerned with simple pleasures and griefs when there's no need to show off, as you call it. That Sylvie often expressed a much more mature state of mind than you're choosing to show me now."

"Really? How utterly boring for you, dear Professor! I do apologize," she said with an artificial little laugh, and he frowned.

"Don't..." he said gently. "There's no need to try to impress me with these charming poses. I did homage to your beauty at that first meeting, now I want to get to know the other Sylvie."

She was silent, not knowing how to counter such an unfamiliar approach, but aware with that warning prick of excitement that she could find him attractive. Had she known a year ago, she thought, that the bearded stranger whose request she had taken so lightly would turn out like this she wouldn't have handed over her commitment so casually to Sarah.

He was looking at her now across the table with an expression she found a shade disturbing and the waiter's arrival with their coffee was a welcome diversion. As she poured the coffee, she found herself wondering if Sarah, too, found him attractive and what the two of them had talked about on the way back from the Fox last night.

"I hope my little cousin entertained you nicely on the way home and didn't go hareing off on the moor looking for more lame ducks," she said, trying to sound merely conversational.

"On the contrary. She offered me her arm up the hill and was most insistent on a rest at the top — one lame duck being enough to be going on with, so to speak," he replied quite gravely, then laughed. "You do your cousin an injustice, you know, if you write her off as a hoydenish child who hasn't grown up."

"Well, she hasn't really. What did you find to talk about?"

"Oh, this and that. She was admitting me just a little, I think, to her own particular freemasonry."

Sylvie's violet eyes opened wide with uncomprehending astonishment.

"What on earth do you mean?" she exclaimed. "I thought Freemasons were a kind of comic secret society who wore aprons and things."

His laughter was quite spontaneous. She was pretty enough and still young enough for him to find charm in artless ignorance, neither did he suppose she was as ingenuous as she would have him believe.

"You must know very well that there are plenty of other kinds. It's only a word to cover the freedom of one's private world," he said, and her eyes lost a little of their soft surprise. With no occasion to seek solace within herself, she had little conception of what he was trying to say, but she remembered Sarah's odd behaviour the day of Adam's arrival and her ridiculous belief that more of herself had gone into those letters than their recipient had any right to. It would be just like Sarah, she thought, to build up some bogus relationship and embarrass the poor man with a schoolgirl crush.

"You mustn't let Sarah's oddities disturb you, Adam," she said, trying to sound adult and amused.

"It's not altogether her fault if she's a little naive at times. There haven't been many young men to take an interest, you see, and it must be hard, sometimes, to take a back seat in your own home."

"Isn't it a little presumptuous to trade on one's superior advantages?" he asked quite gently. "Beauty isn't the sole criterion of perfection, however pleasing it may be to the collector's eye."

"What *do* you mean? Can I help it if poor old Uncle Gil has a bee in his bonnet?"

"No, but you could try taking a back seat yourself every now and again for a change, couldn't you?"

Sylvie might be stupid in some respects, but she had her share of mother wit and a little warning bell was beginning to ring. She was shrewd enough to realize that whether or not he was in love with her, Adam was not blind to Sarah's situation and she thought it more than likely that the plain little cousin had already made good use of her time. Sarah, upon reflection, however, was probably too scrupulous or too dumb to turn matters to her own advantage, but it seemed expedient to scotch any misguided notions she might have put into the Professor's head.

"You don't understand, Adam," she said, leaning confidingly towards him across the table. "I know it must seem very odd to a stranger that my uncle apparently cares more for me than his own daughter, but it's not how it appears. Uncle Gil is a nice old boy if you take him the right way, but a bit bogus, and we all go along with that because it makes life easier. I don't take anything from Sarah that she would want from him, you know. I just please his eye and feed his ego. Sarah doesn't mind — it keeps his attention off her."

"I see," he said, and she made a little rueful grimace at him.

"No, I don't think you do." she retorted. "You think I take advantage of Sarah's plainness, but it isn't like that at all, whatever she may have told you."

"She hasn't told me anything. We're not, as you may have noticed, on very intimate terms," he said with some dryness. She was relieved that her suspicions were, so far, evidently unfounded, but she had no wish to be thought spiteful and said quickly:

"Oh, I didn't imagine, of course, that Sarah would have been complaining — she's not that kind, but I can always manage Uncle Gil and she never could, so really having me to live with them made life easier all round. Will you have some more coffee?"

"No, thanks."

"Then can we go? You promised we could look at the shops after lunch and I'd like to find something pretty for Sarah to make up for being left at home."

They strolled along the pavements looking into shop windows which Adam privately thought a poor way of spending a fine afternoon, but Sylvie's spontaneous pleasure became in itself rewarding and the admiring glances she attracted flattering to any man's ego. When she had found what she wanted for Sarah they set out for home with Adam at the wheel and Sylvie beside him, her thoughts busy with speculation as she chattered away. She had wondered earlier if she had been too hasty in turning down his suggestion of walking to the sea which might have been the opportunity he was seeking to declare himself, but there was always that far more secluded port of call in the Hollow where Granny Coker had her caravan and turned a blind eye to the goings-on of the village courting couples. However, when the car had breasted the hill which met the first fringe of the moor, Adam pulled on to the verge and said unexpectedly: "Let's walk."

She was not shod for walking, having chosen her most elegant shoes to grace a more sartorial occasion, neither was she much enamoured of the moor, but glancing at his dark face with its high-bridged dominant nose and eyes that were no longer quite so cool and dispassionate, she experienced the same little thrill that Nick could rouse in her so easily.

They walked in silence for a while along one of the many sheep-tracks that criss-crossed through the bracken and gorse until they came to a little hollow sheltered from the wind by a rough formation of rock.

"Let us take our ease here for a time while we exchange reminiscences and make discoveries," Adam said with a deliberate lapse into pedantry, and lowering himself on to the turf, stretched up a hand to pull her down beside him.

"How oddly you talk at times — just like a real professor," she said a little uncertainly, and he smiled.

"Not what you're accustomed to in the matter of romantic overtures, perhaps," he replied, and she gave him a puzzled look.

"Is this a romantic overture, then?" she asked, feeling sure of herself again.

"Time will show. There are more ways than one of skinning a cat, so they say."

"Well, *that's* not a very attractive way of putting it! Perhaps you're not very versed in the art of lovemaking, Professor?" she said, hoping to sting him into more familiar methods of declaring himself, but he merely looked quizzical.

"Now that is rather jumping the gun, if you'll forgive a couple of badly mixed metaphors, but since you appear to doubt my talents, let me reassure you," he said, and pulled her into his arms.

His kisses were experimental rather than passionate, she thought, and seemed to match the rather academic flavour of his speech. She responded automatically to a situation she thoroughly understood, but was aware at the same time that things were not quite as they should be. She was both disappointed and a little chagrined when he let her go as abruptly as he had taken her and remarked with rather insulting composure:

"That's enough to be going on with. Do you indulge much in such pleasantries with our friend of last night?"

"Well, of all the nerve!" she exclaimed, angry that her expectations had been brought to such a rude conclusion. "If you're just going through the motions to oblige, like someone handing out sweets to a child, you can think again, Professor! And your technique is lousy, let me tell you!"

He leaned back against the rock, enjoying the warmth of the sun-baked stone on his shoulders, and observed her quizzically.

"You know nothing about my technique, as yet, and you haven't answered my question," he said lazily.

"Nick's in love with me, if that's what you want to know."

"And you?"

"Would you care?"

The lazy look went out of his eyes and his voice became brusque.

"Oh, my dear girl! That's a meaningless question at this stage of affairs," he said impatiently. "I take it that you evidently find the handsome Mr. Bannister's advances to your liking, and who am I to object on that score?"

"But oughtn't you to? I mean surely it's natural — Nick's quite jealous of you."

"Is he, now? And that of course is what last night's pretty little display in the pub was leading up to." Suddenly he laughed and laid a hand over hers for a moment. "Oh, Sylvie, you're so transparent! A spoilt child with a bit of a minx thrown in. You shouldn't need to work so hard for what you can get so easily."

"I don't understand in the least what you're driving at."

"Don't you? Well, I'll tell you this, my charming Circe, if my intentions should turn out to be serious I would not only care very much that you allowed another man privileges that should be mine, but wouldn't stand for it, either. Does that answer you?"

It did not answer her at all, for she was quite unused to such behaviour in a possible suitor. His fashion of making love, if one could call it that, was decidedly tepid when compared with Nick's, and whatever his ultimate intentions she had clearly been precipitate in expecting the day to end with a proposal. She could only take refuge in the one way she knew to turn the tables on him and allowed the easy tears to well up and brim over.

Adam, if impatient with her lack of perception, nevertheless felt remorseful. Sylvie in tears reminded him of Meg who had wept rarely, but with the same heart-catching charm, and he wanted to take her in his arms again and comfort her as he would a child. But instinct warned him that whatever comfort Sylvie desired of him it was not the nursery variety, and he merely patted her hand and said:

"Oh, now, don't be upset. I was only trying to explain that as at present I'm in no position to object, or to interfere in your affairs, the state of my feelings is best left unexpressed. I fancy you've indulged in the breaking of hearts more than is good for you, Miss Deverell!"

"Perhaps," she agreed, smiling at him through her tears with renewed complacency. "But perhaps your heart is more proof than others, Professor?"

"Proof or not, it doesn't break easily," he informed her somewhat disappointingly. "Now dry your eyes and let's get back to the car."

The moment was clearly past for a renewal of intimacies, she thought, as she scrambled to her feet and, observing a laddered stocking and shoes rather the worse for wear, felt decidedly cross. Once more on the road she preserved a sulky silence until as they neared the crossroads when the hill dipped down to Peavey village, she looked out of the window and exclaimed impatiently:

"There's Sarah! I bet that wretched dog of hers is on the loose again. We'd better stop and offer her a lift."

Adam pulled up at the side of the road and watched the running Sarah with interest. She came hurrying towards them, stumbling over the rough places with all the old lack of grace.

"Have you seen Willie?" she called anxiously.

"What did I tell you?" Sylvie said to Adam. "No, of course we haven't," she called back through the open window. "We had better things to do than keep our eyes open for your revolting mongrel. Why can't you see that he's shut up properly?"

"He's not revolting," Sarah said, but it was clearly a protest of long standing and not intended to express indignation. "I did shut him up, but someone must have let him out while I was doing my stint with the spastics. I was going over to Sowton to see if he's there. Will you come with me?"

"I'll come along with you," Adam said, as she turned to run on. "Two are better than one in a search. Sylvie can drive the car back."

"*Will* you?" Sarah said on a rising inflection of surprised pleasure, but Sylvie was not pleased.

"Don't be absurd, Adam! You'll probably crock up that ankle again, and Sarah's quite capable of coping on her own," she said.

"I'm sure she is. Still, it's pleasant to have company when you're a little worried and, as I've already pointed out, two pairs of eyes are better than one," Adam replied, and was out of the car before she could protest again.

Sarah was already walking on, impatient to get going, and as Sylvie slid over to the driver's seat, looking decidedly annoyed, Adam leaned in at the window and chucked her gently under the chin.

56

"Don't spoil a nice day by being childish," he said. "Your cousin really cares about that dog, you know."

Sarah was waiting for him at a point where the track divided.

"You had no need to come, you know," she said a little shyly. "Are you sure your ankle will stand rough going?"

"Perfectly sure if I take it slowly," he replied. "I'm quite used to trekking, you know."

"Yes, of course. I was forgetting you've explored strange places and forgotten civilizations," she said absently, and he gave her a quick glance.

"That's a curious remark."

"Is it? But that must surely be half the fascination of your expeditions — discovering the unknown, I mean."

"Yes, it is, and I only meant curious in the sense that your cousin used almost the self-same phrase in one of her letters. Perhaps you have an affinity over some things."

"Oh!" she said a little blankly, then began to call and whistle for Willie. "You'd better go that way, Adam, and I'll circle round to the right. We'll meet at the farm."

He was first at the meeting place and leaned on the little clapper bridge looking down into the brown peaty water which bubbled noisily over the rocky shallows, scarcely wide or deep enough to be called a river. Contentment filled him, listening to the hypnotic sound of running water, and he reflected with faint regret on time wasted in a smart hotel which bred only the superficialities of small talk. He must, he thought with tenderness, coax his wayward Sylvie back to the mood of those letters when she had finished trying to impress him with a display of sophistication.

"Hi!" Sarah's shout had come unexpectedly from the farmhouse which, after all, she must have arrived at first, and the next minute she had leapt over the low wall with Willie beside her on a long piece of rope.

"I've got him!" she shouted, hurling herself against the stone parapet beside Adam where she leaned supporting herself and getting back her breath.

"They had him shut up in the shippen all the time but couldn't let us know because they aren't on the phone. They think he's probably mated with their wretched bitch, but they agree it's their own fault for not keeping her in and I'm going to have one of the pups." Oh, Adam, it's such a relief! You don't know what I suffer on these occasions imagining Farmer Rowe lurking behind a gorse-bush with a gun, waiting to wreak vengeance."

"Does the dog run sheep, then? That could be serious."

"It was never proved. He was just a stray that nobody wanted and used to tag on to any roving dog that would let him. There was a big black lurcher that came from the gypsy encampment over at Yammerton which no one could catch and one day Rowe spotted them both in amongst his flock. The lurcher got away, but Willie lost an eye and I found him half-dead in the Hollow where Granny had taken him in. It took weeks of patience to gain his confidence, and Rowe tried to make trouble. He couldn't do much except threaten, of course, as Willie at last had a proper home, but he swore he'd shoot him if he ever caught him straying near his land, and he's a mean-tempered man who'd shoot first and find out later."

She stooped to take the rope off Willie. The dog bounded away barking hysterically, scattering a group of grazing ponies who kicked up their heels and galloped away and Sarah sped after them.

Adam, following more slowly, watched her flying figure springing sure-footed over the rough ground, and had the strange impression that she was running away from him. He was, he found to his surprise, sorely tempted to pursue and catch her, and but for the handicap of his damaged ankle, might well have done so.

"When will you take me to throw coins to the pixies?" he asked, catching up with her as she paused on the shoulder of moorland which dropped down to Slattery.

"You should get Sylvie to take you if you want your wishes to come true," she answered a little primly.

"Why? Is her influence with the Little People greater than yours?"

"Oh, no, it's just that it's mostly courting couples who visit the pool and the piskies are more likely to oblige by spiriting away your coins if you go there with your true love."

"More likely Granny Coker with an eye to future benefits!" he retorted, and caught her suddenly by the shoulder. "Are you by any chance playing games with me, Sarah?"

She did not pull away, but her freckled face looked suddenly young and uncertain in the gathering dusk.

"Games?" she echoed, trying to recapture a diminishing sense of achievement, but the failing light, the silence and scents of the moor and Adam's restraining hand on her shoulder recalled too vividly the emotions of last night and her new-found confidence was lost.

"Yes, games, young woman. You're either a little fey as a result of snatching the unspeakable Willie from the jaws of death or you're presuming a trifle prematurely on matters which shouldn't concern you."

"Then it's probably that — Willie, I mean, and you don't know him well enough to call him unspeakable," she said, breaking away. "I'm sorry if I'm poking my nose in where it isn't wanted, but you can hardly blame me if I'm concerned for my cousin."

"And are you?"

No, she wanted to shout at him, *I'm concerned for you, you dope, because Sylvie isn't at all the sort of person you've imagined and I'm afraid you'll be hurt . . .*

"Of course," she said instead, then thanking him sedately for his help in looking for Willie, turned abruptly and raced off down the track to the house.

CHAPTER IV

SHE did not bother to change since she never wore slacks when on duty at the Home, neither did she do more to make herself presentable beyond washing off the day's dust and running a comb through her hair. She sat with her family, silent and a little withdrawn, hoping to make it clear to the Professor that she had no intention of taking advantage of his friendly overtures, but she was uncomfortably aware of her cousin's eyes upon her with a new alertness which suggested that she was harbouring speculations which did not altogether please her.

Sylvie wore her kaftan and had twisted her hair into a complicated arrangement on the crown of her head. She looked enchanting and very elegant and if Adam's eyes were occasionally a little amused as though he was well aware that she was deliberately setting out to charm him, charmed he clearly was, and no wonder, thought Sarah, feeling suddenly plain and rather cross.

Gilbert, presiding seriously over the dinner-table and directing the talk along channels that best suited his own conversational talents, looked none the less with a fond eye upon his niece and his attentive guest and when, the meal finished, he and Adam were left to their port and cigars, he considered the time had arrived for a little delicate probing.

"And what are your immediate plans, my dear fellow?" he enquired blandly. "Another expedition to untrammelled lands?"

"Nothing like that just yet," Adam replied, "but I have a commission to authenticate a new development relating to china-clay in parts of Cornwall which brought me down here in the first place, as I think I told you, so I must be moving on soon."

"Oh, my dear chap! I was not intending to imply we want to get rid of you, and I had thought, I must confess, that this project you mentioned was something in the nature of an excuse for your visit," Gilbert said a little roguishly. "I trust you aren't thinking of leaving us just yet — we're just getting to know you."

"That's very kind of you, sir, but I mustn't impose on your hospitality. In a week or so my colleagues will be down here ready to start work, but perhaps I may be allowed to keep in touch at week-ends? I shall only be in the next county."

"Of course, of course, but why not make Slattery your headquarters? If you have a car laid up anywhere it would be nothing to commute between here and the Duchy and very much more comfortable for you than some country pub."

Adam was not a vain man, but his host's eagerness to keep him could hardy be misinterpreted.

"Very much nicer if you still feel the same when the time comes," he replied courteously. "I mean to look about for a decent used car in any case, as I sold my old one rather than have the expense of laying it up for a year."

"Excellent, excellent! You couldn't do better than try Banks in Tawstock — of course it's Bannister now, but one can't keep up with this modern trend for mergers and take-overs, can one? That gay young spark of Sylvie's owns the firm, I understand, so they should be able to fix you up with something reliable. Have you met young Bannister?"

"Yes. I understand he's married." Adam sounded noncommittal, but Gilbert gave him a shrewd look.

"Yes, alas, though I gather the marriage has broken up. We don't approve, of course, and I won't have the fellow to the house while he's still tied up, but it would be foolish to stop them meeting, mm'm?"

"Then you wouldn't refuse your consent should your

niece wish to marry him if the divorce goes through?"

"Well, now, that's a tricky question," Gilbert said, looking mischievous. "I don't deny that I would prefer my lovely Sylvie to choose a husband who was not, shall we say, second-hand goods, but there are few eligible *partis* around here and in these modern times one cannot afford to be too selective, mm'm?"

There was something specious about this argument, Adam thought, and he said casually:

"You are anxious to see your niece settled early, I take it."

Gilbert examined his hands with minute concentration.

"On the contrary, she is a constant delight to my eye — a veritable *objet d'art* which I shall be disolated to part with, but selfish desires must give way to expediency, alas," he said whimsically.

"Expediency?"

"Yes, yes ... whatever my personal inclinations, I cannot rob my own flesh and blood, can I? This house is held in trust for Sarah and goes to her on my death with her mother's small capital, so I cannot provide for Sylvie as I would wish. It is fortunate, in the circumstances, is it not, that Mother Nature has provided her with such lavish compensation?"

"You are suggesting, I take it, that by comparison, your daughter's chances are slender," said Adam, his attention clicking into focus again, and Gilbert allowed himself a small grimace of rueful humour.

"Well, my dear chap, I should have thought that was obvious. The poor child can't help being plain, of course, but she doesn't make much effort to cultivate other charms, you must agree."

"Does one cultivate charm?" Adam parried lightly. "I would have thought it was a quality which defies being pinned down to anything so specific."

"Yes, perhaps. Well, we're all unfortunately as we are

made, and my ugly duckling was just unlucky when the fairies attended her christening. Why are you looking at me like that, my dear fellow? You're surely not going to stretch politeness to the point of assuring me untruthfully that you don't find my daughter plain?"

"No, I wasn't going to do that, but shall we leave your daughter out of this? It's none of my business, in any case, to advance opinions," Adam said quietly, and Gilbert's neat white beard quivered in the candlelight as he laughed a little selfconsciously.

"Of course it isn't. Your business has been with our delectable little siren right from the beginning, has it not?" he said effusively. "I don't mind telling you now that both Frances and I were extremely surprised that our fickle jade had stuck to her bargain. Sylvie is no letter-writer in the ordinary way, so I think you can congratulate yourself for being one up on the fascinating Mr. Bannister ... now I'm embarrassing you by letting my fond speculations run away with me. Have some more port?"

Sarah had gone when they went back to the parlour. She did not come back and at ten o'clock Gilbert announced a little self-consciously that he was going to bed and would Frances please put the cats out now, then bring him up a glass of hot milk.

"You'll see to the lamps, won't you, Soames?" he said at the door, and went out, leaving it rather ostentatiously ajar.

Left alone, Sylvie stretched lazily and said with a giggle:

"Aren't they sweet? Do you mind, Adam, having your duties pointed out so obviously?"

"My duties?"

"Well, I hope you aren't going to oblige just as a polite return for hospitality, but we haven't been left all alone in the firelight to settle down to a nice game of tiddly-winks."

He made no attempt to get out of his chair, b̶ there with his shoulders comfortably hunched, wa the firelight catch the shimmering threads of the k when she moved, aware of a swift change of mo her and a very definite air of invitation. She was a once adult and assured with a hint of experience he not expected, as if she was aware that she had pla her cards badly in the afternoon.

"You're a curious mixture," he said slowly.

"Am I? But you don't really know me, do you? Y mustn't go too much on those silly letters, you know."

"I wasn't thinking of the letters, as it happens. Th afternoon you were just a rather spoilt little girl bein given a chance to show off her pretty clothes and b admired, and now—"

"Well, what am I now?"

"I'm wondering."

"For an attractive man who one must assume has some experience of women, you're a little slow off th mark, Professor. Why don't you come over and fin out?"

She saw one eyebrow lift quizzically, but he still di not move.

"No, no, Eve. You don't catch me with that old ga I'm a bit more fly than my namesake," he said lazi and she sprang to her feet with an angry little cry a stood there with her back to him.

"How — how c-could you?" she stammered, and realized to his astonishment that she was crying. He get up then and stood behind her feeling a little help

"For heaven's sake! I was only pulling your leg, said.

"You weren't! You think I'm trying to c-catch

"What nonsense! Still, don't you think you're trying to jump the gun?"

"I don't know what you mean."

No, she didn't, he thought with faint exasp

65

she was a little girl again; a little girl who was so accustomed to masculine capitulation that she could not understand a more subtle approach.

"I mean that there are some things which shouldn't be forced," he said patiently, but he had chosen the wrong words again.

"Who's forcing you?" she demanded angrily. "The men I've known haven't needed any prodding to show interest. Don't you find me attractive?"

"If all you want from me is an assurance of masculine virility, come here," he retorted with sudden impatience, and swung her round into his arms.

She looked up into his dark face and saw the deep lines about his mouth tighten to darker furrows and she gave a little sigh of satisfaction and slid her arms round his neck. He could feel the tears still wet on her cheeks to remind him of his clumsiness as he kissed her, but her mouth was eager and knowledgeable under his and the sudden pressure of her breasts warm and hard. He did not know why, when he released her, he should feel a measure of disappointment, unless, he thought wryly, he had misinterpreted those letters, but it was hardly reasonable to quarrel with the reality because of a falsely conceived image...

Sarah, who had come downstairs for an apple, saw them through the half-open door and, experiencing a most irrational moment of pain, fled back to her room and slammed the door shut. She lay awake for a long time listening to the owls calling from the orchard and regretting that she so seldom was able to relieve her sore spirit with tears.

By morning the weather had changed with that suddenness which always surprises when there is no gentle bridging between the seasons. Summer had been banished overnight and sheets of rain and a blustery wind which stripped the last leaves from the orchard had

turned the moor to bleakness.

"Well, one must remember we're into October. It's been such a wonderful summer right up to the end of September that one has scarcely noticed it's autumn," Frances said at breakfast, and Sarah looked at the streaming windows and thought nostalgically of those halcyon days gone for ever with the last of summer. In a way it seemed fitting when so much of her private world had been jettisoned too, then she remembered her childhood when the summer had seemed too long waiting for the traditional delights of Goose Fair.

"What are you grinning at? There's nothing very funny about this stinking day?" Sylvie said crossly. She had planned an elaborate outfit for the morning's excursion which was to present her with such a splendid opportunity for playing one admirer off against the other under her own roof, but it looked as if it would have to be mackintoshes and stout shoes instead.

"I was thinking of Goosey," Sarah replied. "Shall you come this year, Sylvie, to show the Professor the sights, or are you still too superior?"

"I'm not superior — just selective," Sylvie said a little sharply. "Possibly Adam doesn't share your naive enthusiasm for bucolic junketings."

"On the contrary, I can never resist a fair, so I hope you'll humour us both and step down to our level," Adam said with a twinkle, and she gave him a suspicious look.

"Well, in that case we'll make up a party. Nick will come if I ask him nicely," she said.

"And if I ask you nicely will you ride a cock horse with me, having, of course, rings on your fingers and bells on your toes?" Adam said, and she looked puzzled.

"What? Oh, you mean the roundabouts. Sarah's the one for that. They make me feel sick."

"Really? I seem to remember you saying — well,

67

never mind. Perhaps you'll take pity on me then, Sarah? It's no fun to go whirling round on a fiery charger by oneself."

"No, it isn't, is it? Yes, of course, Adam, if it would amuse you," Sarah answered rather sedately, but pleasure bubbled up in her. It would, she thought, be something rather special to spin round on a painted horse with the Professor behind, holding her firmly in case she fell off.

"Well, I shall stay on the ground and jeer. Grown-up people look so silly larking about like kids," said Sylvie, sounding annoyed.

"Children, not kids, if you please — a dreadful word when not applied to young goats," her uncle interposed rather absently from behind his paper.

"That only shows how young you are," Adam said, smiling at the face she made at her uncle. "When you've reached my age, there's a perverse enjoyment in returning to one's youth."

"All right, Methuselah, if that's how you feel, but I shall still jeer," Sylvie retorted, but her annoyance vanished and she gave him a little secret smile to remind him, no doubt, thought Sarah, that however off-hand she might sound, last night's little episode was a bond between them and not forgotten.

Nick arrived punctually with a Rover 200 in excellent condition which he assured Adam he could vouch for personally. They set out without Sarah, Sylvie relegated to the back seat, and the trial run proving entirely satisfactory, they stopped at the garage in Tawstock on the way home to complete the details of sale. Sylvie was looking a little sulky when they arrived back at Slattery, Nick having, to Adam's amusement, dealt very expertly with irrelevant feminine interruptions. At luncheon she had little opportunity for practising the provocations which had been so successful that evening at the Fox, for Nick, whatever his private inclinations, was too well-mannered and too astute to ignore his host. Indeed he made himself so agreeable that when he had gone, Gilbert said complacently:

"Not a bad young fellow at all. Excellent manners and a surprising amount of sound general knowledge. What did you make of him, Soames?"

"A clever operator, I would guess," Adam replied a little absently. He had been wondering with some surprise why he should feel such little concern over Sylvie's attachment for the young man. He had thought it a pity that she had become involved with someone whose matrimonial prospects were still a matter of conjecture, but jealousy was not part of it.

"Are you suggesting the fellow's a shark?" Gilbert asked, frowning, and Adam looked surprised.

"Certainly not," he replied. "I simply meant that he struck me as a typical example of the shrewd young business executive who doesn't miss a trick. He wouldn't, I fancy, allow his heart to rule his head if it meant sacrificing his ambitions, but that's an essential quality these days if you mean to succeed in big business."

"Dear me! Are you a cynic?" Gilbert said a little patronisingly.

"I don't think so. Wasn't it Wilde who said a cynic is a man who knows the price of everything but the value of nothing?" Adam replied with a smile, and Gilbert, who considered apt quotations to be his province, looked annoyed.

"Yes, yes," he said petulantly. "A very overrated writer with a reputation for cheap epigrams, I've always thought. Now, my dear fellow, what are you going to do with yourself for the rest of the afternoon? It was a little inconsiderate of my naughty niece to decide at the last minute to drive back with Bannister and waste time in a cinema, but you mustn't let it upset you. Feminine machinations, you know."

The roguish implication was so plain that Adam found himself answering more shortly than he intended.

"It would seem to me a very sensible way of spending a wet afternoon, but don't feel put out on my account, sir. I shall probably go for a walk," he said, and made his escape.

Sarah had already made her own escape to the stable-room, not wishing to be ordered by her father to enter-tain the guest, who possibly had no wish to be burdened with her company. She lit the ancient and rather rickety paraffin stove which was the sole means of heating, provided Willie with an old marrow-bone to keep him quiet, then curled herself up in an armchair to ruminate.

She reached for the topmost volume of the pile of exercise books which contained her journal and sadly turned the pages. Now that the letters no longer occu-pied her spare moments she had returned to the old avenue of escape.

"Hi! May I come up?" Adam's voice called suddenly from the bottom of the stairs, making her jump and she hurriedly pushed the journal out of sight. He did not wait for a reply and she could hear him mounting the wooden steps outside.

"Of course stay if you would like," she said politely. "You'd better have this chair, the other one's got a broken spring."

"Don't get up, this will do me," he said, propping himself on the edge of the table. "I'm still a stranger to you, aren't I, Sarah? I wonder why you're so prickly."

No, not a stranger, she thought, feeling the colour mount under her skin; how could he ever be that when he already knew so many of her thoughts? Suddenly it seemed entirely right that he should be sitting here in this room where she had written to him and conjured up so many images and dreamed so many foolish dreams.

"Prickly — but I'm not really. I just have an awk-ward way with me, as Father would be the first to tell

70

you," she replied, and he shook his head at her.

"You should be used to your father's omissions by now," he said humorously. "We can't altogether help our blind spots, you know."

"Don't you like Father?" she asked with surprise, and he evaded the question by asking another.

"You don't resent your cousin's attractions, do you?"

"Certainly not!" she snapped, sounding slightly outraged. "Like all men, I suppose you can't believe that a woman can admire another without feeling jealous of her superior charms."

"I'm not quite so thick-skulled as that, but it was a silly question. I had been going to add when you snapped my head off that there was no need. You have plenty of charm of your own when you forget your prickles," he said, and she coloured again. "Now, let's stop talking at cross-purposes. I'm very conscious that I've trespassed on your private preserves, but I hope you'll show forgiveness by letting me into some of your secrets."

"My s-secrets?" she stammered, thinking for one horrifying moment that he had somehow stumbled on the truth about the letters.

"This room is full of secrets — or perhaps I should have said childhood treasures and mementoes — like those nursery books and the china animals on the shelf, and that intriguing collection of flints and quartz which naturally attracts my professional eye. I was only asking to be allowed to share."

Quite suddenly her reservations melted away in a rush of affection for him. Had she not all her childhood wanted to share her private gods, only to learn very early that the values of others were different from one's own? She remembered now quite vividly the pain and indignation she had felt at Gloriana's rejection, and laughed aloud.

"Was that so funny?" Adam asked, sounding a little

disappointed and she hastened to reassure him.

"I wasn't laughing at you wanting to share — that was kind and made me feel warm all over. I was remembering a doll I treasured and tried to give to Sylvie when she first came to live with us and how hurt I was when she didn't want her and said she was ugly. She was, too, only until that moment I'd thought her beautiful."

"Because you loved her, of course. Poor Sarah! Children can be fiendishly cruel sometimes. Used you to quarrel much?"

"No, not much. Sylvie never wanted the sort of things I did, so there was no occasion for the usual childish squabbles over property. Besides, it was always Sylvie who ended up in tears, and then I would feel a worm all over again."

He gave her a quick, amused glance.

"I take it the lady cries easily, then?" he said, and she laughed.

"Oh, yes. Sylvie's tears used to upset us all very much at first, but we learnt not to take them too much to heart — even Father. She does it so beautifully that you can only admire and give in."

She became aware that he was looking at her with rather a curious expression and had the uncomfortable feeling that he thought her remarks a little spiteful.

"Don't get the wrong idea," she said quickly. "I wasn't having a dig at Sylvie, only stating a fact. She doesn't do it on purpose to get sympathy, you know. She just can't help herself when something upsets her."

"I see. It doesn't do in this world to be over-sensitive," he said, and she imagined he sounded a shade reproving. It was no good telling him that Sylvie might be over-sensitive on her own account but was delightfully unaware of the more tender feelings of others, but she hoped he would not find this out for himself and be unprepared.

The time seemed to slip away unnoticed as they sat

and talked and only the dwindling daylight reminded Sarah that the hour must be getting late. It was so easy to ask questions and give answers in the shadows broken only by the pale ring of light from the stove and the occasional flare of a match when Adam relit his pipe. She did not afterwards remember very much what they talked about, but learnt something of his early background. His mother had died when he was a boy, he said; his father, who was clearly loved and admired, had died a few years later, and he himself went through the usual channels of public school and university, finishing up with a high degree in mineralogy. He seemed to have made few intimate friends in the process of growing up and it sounded to Sarah a lonely and rather sad approach to manhood, but Adam only laughed when she ventured to say so.

"Lonely, perhaps at times, but not sad," he said. "Money wasn't short, fortunately, and later I got tremendous satisfaction out of my job and particularly these far expeditions. Like you, I'm something of a cat that walks by itself."

"Like me?"

"Well, you are, aren't you?"

"Yes, perhaps. It's a good thing to be under some conditions."

"Yes, but there comes a time, you know. There is always a complementary second half somewhere around if you have the luck to run across them."

"And you think Sylvie —" she began incautiously, but if he heard the astonishment in her voice he ignored it.

"It wasn't your cousin I had in mind just then," he replied. "My second half was a girl called Meg. We were going to be married about a couple of years ago."

"Oh!" she said a little blankly. "Why didn't you — get married, I mean?"

"She died. She had a mild attack of 'flu one winter

73

like so many other people, but she had a weak heart which no one had suspected and she died."

"Oh, *Adam*!"

"Don't feel sorry. We had so much during those few short months and I've nothing to regret. That's the answer to grief, Sarah, you know. If you can look back with no regrets for quarrels, misunderstandings, things that are best left unsaid, you have nothing to trouble memories that can only be happy ones."

"I don't think I could ever feel that way," said Sarah rather wretchedly. To her it seemed terrible that having seemingly had so little from human relationships, his time of fulfilment should have been so brief.

"But then you're young," he told her with gentle mockery. "At your age one expects so much and has so little experience of life as it has to be lived."

"I don't expect anything," she said rather bleakly, adding curiously: "What was she like?"

He had let his pipe go out and was silent for a moment while he got it going again. She watched the little flame spring up, casting alternate light and shadow on his face, giving it a look of withdrawal, and she wondered if she had trespassed in asking the question.

"To look at?" he said then, and there was nothing in his voice but an untroubled willingness to talk. "So like your cousin that for a moment I thought I was seeing a ghost."

His reply was so unexpected, so completely at variance to anything she had imagined that she could only stammer out her next words.

"Then ... then ... you only fell in love with an image ... not with Sylvie at all," she said, and he cocked a quizzical eyebrow at her.

"I don't know that falling in love is quite the right definition," he said. "I seem to remember telling you at our very first meeting that love at first sight was strictly for the young and untried."

74

"Yes, you did, but I thought you were just putting me in my place for being nosey."

"Did you, Sarah? Well, perhaps you seemed to me to be having romantic ideas that could be misleading."

"Then — then weren't you serious?"

His air of casual amusement left him as he made reply: "Oh, yes, I was quite serious — not so much in following up an impulse of the moment, but in a quest for confirmation. The letters were a link, you see, with that other ghost, and I came back to find out."

"Find out what?"

"Whether one initial coincidence had set me on a false trail to build up an image which didn't exist — whether being cut off from civilisation for months on end I had perhaps read too much into those letters."

"But they weren't love letters," she said unguardedly, and although she thought he glanced at her rather sharply it was now too dark for him to see her face.

"No, they weren't love letters in the accepted sense," he said. "But love came through — the basic love which we all have as children, and somehow lose when we get older ... but perhaps I'm just being fanciful."

"Yes, I expect you are," Sarah said, and got up abruptly.

The room seemed suddenly unbearably stuffy with the paraffin fumes and she went to open the window. What had she done, keeping alive an image which did not exist outside herself? she wondered, leaning out into the darkness to breathe in the fresh damp air. She felt instinctively that this accidental likeness could be no more than superficial, but how far would a man, blinded by coincidence into fashioning a dream, look below the surface?

The light of a torch bobbing up and down in the darkness distracted her thoughts and the next moment Sylvie's voice called up from the yard:

"Sarah! Is the Professor up there with you? Aunt

Fran's wondering if he went out on the moor and got lost."

"Yes, he's here," Sarah answered, and caught the staccato exasperation in the sound of Sylvie's footsteps mounting the wooden stairs. There was no time to light the lamp, and Willie, rudely awakened from his slumbers, sprang across the room in the darkness barking his usual defiance. Sylvie gave a little scream as she opened the door and drew back.

"The brute's bitten me! I knew he would one day — call him off, Sarah. You ought to have him put down, he's dangerous!" she cried.

Sarah hauled the dog back to his corner while Adam, with admirable promptness, found and lighted the lamp.

"If only you'd speak to him when you come bursting in he'd realise you're a friend," Sarah said. "He knows you don't like him."

"And when should I when all he wants is to take a piece out of me? And this time he has. I shall tell Uncle Gil!"

"Let me look — why, there isn't a mark!"

"Well, he's torn my stockings and it's no fault of his that he didn't break the skin," Sylvie snapped, but the shrillness had gone from her voice and she sent a quick, uneasy glance in Adam's direction. She had not meant to make such a fuss, but the dog had startled her. Her afternoon with Nick had ended in a quarrel and it was distinctly galling to find Adam up here and in no need of the consolation she had been prepared to offer.

Something in the expression on his face bent over the lamp as he turned up the wick gave her the feeling that she had been over-confident, and as her gaze passed to Sarah and noted her flushed face and the unruly state of her hair, she said:

"Well! How long have you two been sitting here in the dark? It's hardly much fun for our guest, Sarah, to be dragged up to a smelly loft that stinks like a zoo."

"On the contrary," Adam said smoothly, "I invited myself, and I can assure you the time was well spent."

The look of surprise in Sylvie's eyes changed slowly to one of unwilling comprehension.

"Oh, I see — on the principle of what's sauce for the goose, I suppose," she said, but he merely looked amused.

"If you're alluding to yourself then you certainly are a goose," he said good-humouredly. "Was the cinema unproductive, by any chance?"

"I don't know what you're talking about," she replied angrily.

"I was referring to the film, naturally. It's always disappointing when the picture doesn't come up to scratch, or you find you've seen it before," Adam said, and Sarah, despite her embarrassment, smiled. Sylvie saw the smile and rightly interpreted it.

"You *do* look a mess, darling," she said solicitously. "You should have come to the flicks with us instead of boxing yourself up with your smelly animals."

"You didn't ask me," Sarah pointed out with truth, and Adam remarked, gazing absently at the ceiling: "I may be an animal in the biological sense, but I hope I'm not smelly."

Sarah could not stop herself from giving way to giggles, and Sylvie flounced out of the room and down the steps without another word. Sarah could hear her running across the cobbles and the angry slam of the iron gate leading into the garden, and her merriment died. It was so seldom that Sylvie ever got the worst of an encounter that she began to feel guilty.

"It wasn't very kind to let her go like that, was it, Adam?" she said. "I think she's probably had a row with Nick and was getting some of her own back."

"Very likely," he replied, piling the cups and saucers together and emptying ashtrays. "Don't feel anxious, you tender-hearted creature. I'm well enough

77

acquainted with feminine quirks not to be put off by childish behaviour. Sylvie and I have a lot of ground to cover before coming to an adult understanding."

"But your Meg wasn't like that, was she?" Sarah said, tossing corn to the crow which had made a nest for itself in one of her discarded hats.

"No," he replied thoughtfully, "Meg was more like you, now I come to think of it, but then her parents were wise, and didn't spoil her, so one must be tolerant. Your cousin, on the other hand, doesn't seem to have been given much chance of forgetting herself, and I fancy the real Sylvie comes through when her only audience is an inanimate typewriter."

"Oh, hell! Those blasted letters!" Sarah exclaimed before she had time to think, and he put out the stove and the lamp and began striking matches to light them to the door.

"Yes," he said, piloting her across the room, "those blasted letters present quite an interesting problem in human behaviour, don't they? People seldom realise how much of themselves they reveal when they can let themselves go on paper without fear of reprisals."

She made no reply except to order him rather peremptorily down the steps so that she could lock up for the night, but when she reached the yard she found he had not waited for her. He was, she supposed, already regretting his refusal to side with Sylvie and was hurrying back to the house to make amends.

CHAPTER V

As the time drew nearer for Adam to join the surveying party in Cornwall, his private decision to make his headquarters there rather than at Slattery strengthened. He was, he thought, becoming too much an accepted member of the family for his own comfort; his host's expansive manner suggested an air of satisfied anticipation that was growing a little embarrassing, and Sylvie persisted in her needless provocation, blowing hot and cold with exasperating regularity. Sarah could have told him that one of Sylvie's favourite maxims was that a man must never be sure of you, but Sarah was not offering any unsolicited advice, neither, to his chagrin, did she display much enthusiasm for his company.

She would have been very surprised to know that her behaviour troubled Adam rather more than her cousin's predictable skirmishings, but she was giving Sylvie no opportunities for a further cheapening of her private dreams. She withdrew with greater frequency to the safety of the stable-room and purged her uncomfortable emotions in the pages of her journal.

Adam, respecting another's reservations, made no attempt to break them down, but with Frances Deverell, who of all of them he knew so little, he could talk without fear of emotional misconceptions.

"She's like a child wanting to impress the grown-ups with her popularity," he told her impatiently after Sylvie had cancelled yet another arrangement at the last moment and taken herself off with Nick Bannister. "Does she really believe such obvious gambits bring results?"

"They usually have in the past," Frances replied

dryly. "Possibly you aren't sufficiently involved to react in the expected manner.

He glanced at her with interest. She of all of them had never appeared to take his intentions for granted, and he had often wondered what she really thought.

"It's difficult to become involved with a personality that perpetually eludes one, and I'm not a callow boy to fall head over ears in love with just a pretty face," he said, and she smiled.

"No, I don't think you are. I can well imagine that you might have been bowled over by Sylvie's exceptional looks on the eve of departure into comparative exile, but I fancy you're feeling a little let down, now."

"Well, that's hardly Sylvie's fault, is it? I suppose I built too much on those letters. I expected to find a person who didn't really exist."

They were in the little room which Frances used for miscellaneous jobs and writing letters and she was making a flower arrangement of beech leaves and great shaggy chrysanthemums. She paused for a moment, absently stroking her cheek with one of the blooms.

"I've always thought those letters were out of character," she said, and he raised an eyebrow.

"Did you, Miss Deverell? Why?"

"Well, Sylvie's enthusiasms are usually short-lived, once the novelty's worn off, and we none of us suspected that she was still keeping up the correspondence, until you wrote to my brother asking, very properly, to pay your respects. We evidently did her an injustice."

"Perhaps you did. There's something that puzzles me all the same."

"About the letters?"

"Yes, in a sense, but possibly the simple explanation lies in the fact that for some it's easier to reveal oneself in the written word. She inherits something of your brother's literary ability, perhaps?"

"Oh, no, that's Sarah's line of country."

"Sarah?"

"She's always scribbling — spends hours in the stable-room writing a journal none of us are allowed to read, but I daresay that's as far as her literary efforts go. My brother is a bit of a humbug, as you've doubtless guessed," Frances said crisply, returning to her flower arrangement. "He might have achieved more recognition in that field if he'd had to live on his earnings, but he's a born dilettante and manages very nicely on the strength of his early successes."

"You sound bitter," he said, wondering how she had managed to subdue her mind to an obviously inferior intelligence all these years, but she gave him one of the rare smiles that momentarily robbed her face of plainness and said gently:

"Not bitter, Mr. Soames, just realistic. I'm devoted to Gilbert, despite his little pretences, and you mustn't judge him too harshly. In some ways he's still adolescent, you know."

"Yes, I see. If Sylvie was his daughter and not his niece that could explain a lot."

"Well, uncle and niece aren't so far removed that inherited traits need cause surprise. Do you find Sylvie adolescent, then?"

He smiled. "In some ways, but she's been spoilt, hasn't she? Spoilt children tend to grow up slowly. It would seem a pity, however, that your brother appears unable to find a use for his daughter's qualities. I would think little Sarah has quite a lot to give."

Frances made no immediate comment but stood back to observe the effect of her handiwork with a critical eye. Adam thought the bronze and yellows of the turning leaves and the tawny ragged blooms reflected a like quality of richness in her, a quality shared with the young Sarah, and she said then as if he had spoken aloud:

"No one's ever really troubled to explore Sarah's capacity for loving, but it's not entirely Gilbert's fault. He worships beauty and must have perfection. That gives him a blind spot."

"But you, Miss Deverell, if you see so much, surely —"

"Oh, no," she replied, cutting him short, "Sarah and I are alike in some respects, you know. We are too much alike not to be shy of one another's emotions, but Sarah will find her right niche one day. Two plain spinsters ministering to the needs of one old widower would be excessive."

"Do you find Sarah plain?"

"Well, don't you?"

"No, I don't think so. There's something rather endearing about that odd little face — to say nothing of the disparaging freckles!"

She smiled, her eyes resting on him thoughtfully for a moment, then she removed one of the blooms from the copper bowl to shorten the stem and replaced it carefully.

"I'm glad you're not entirely blinded by Sylvie's beauty," she said. "My brother, of course, thinks his daughter's matrimonial chances are slender."

"Why on earth should he?"

"Because, I imagine, she wouldn't appeal to him as a woman. Gilbert tends to judge all men by himself, you know. He would sooner see Sarah leaving home for a husband than Sylvie, of course, but he can't provide for both girls adequately at his death and Sarah, after all, is his daughter. With Sylvie settled and out of the way, there's more chance for Sarah, though, of course, that's my opinion and not Gilbert's. Is it next week you start on your survey, Mr. Soames?"

He suspected she was deliberately changing the subject, a little embarrassed, perhaps, by such uncharacteristic confidences, but it gave him the opening he wanted.

"Yes," he said, "I've been meaning to speak to your

82

brother who very kindly suggested I make my headquarters here, but I think on the whole that it would be more convenient to doss down somewhere on the spot. There's quite a good little pub where the others will be billeted, I understand, and you wouldn't be disturbed by my probably erratic hours."

"You must, of course, suit yourself in that respect," she replied. "Your comings and goings wouldn't put us out if that's what's troubling you, but I don't doubt you have other and sounder reasons." There was no curiosity in her voice, just a statement of fact. Whatever her private thoughts she would never, he knew, try to force a confidence from him. She was, he decided, quite a remarkable woman in her quiet way, and found himself wondering why she had never married.

"Thank you," he said. "If you will be kind enough to have me I would always appreciate the odd week-end."

"Of course. Perhaps, if your plans remain uncertain you would care to come back to us for Christmas?"

"Christmas!" he exclaimed with quite genuine surprise. This year summer had clung with such unusual tenacity to the heels of autumn that it was difficult to realize that winter was almost upon them.

"Yes, I know. It's been such a wonderful summer that one forgets how time slips by. Goose Fair has come round again and that always marks the start of a new season. Are you going to let yourself be inveigled into all the fun of the fair?"

"Of course he is!" Sarah's voice replied unexpectedly from the doorway. "You said you'd ride a cock horse with me, Professor."

She came into the room looking, Adam thought, charmingly boyish in her green slacks, a bright handkerchief knotted at her throat and her brown hair curling closely over her head. She seemed to have temporarily shed her reservations where he was concerned, or perhaps a reminder of the fair was sufficient to make her forget.

"I shall be most happy to oblige a fellow addict," he said. "Are you any good at the rifle range? I'm rather a dab hand myself."

"Then you can win me all those lovely prizes that look so enticing till you get them home. Meanwhile, would you like to come for a walk now with Willie and me? Sylvie won't be back for ages."

"I'd like it very much," he replied gravely. "Perhaps you'll take me to the pixie pool. I have a persistent itch to cast my coins and establish a link with your moorland gods."

"Now you're laughing at me," she said, but without resentment, and her aunt ruffled the back of her head before carefully picking up the bowl of leaves and flowers.

"You do that — there's never any harm in propitiating the gods," she said, walking to the door.

"No, there isn't, is there?"

"You can propitiate Granny at the same time with a pound of tea; there's nothing like keeping on the right side of the oracle. I'll tell Hattie," Frances said, and left the room.

For Sarah the day blossomed into delight. It was stealing nothing from Sylvie to allow herself pleasure in the company of a man who seemed so ready to share in a private world which meant nothing to her cousin. The moor was looking its best with the autumn sunshine sharpening the colours that were more often hidden in mist. Splashes of green and bronze and purple stretched away into a jagged frieze of distant tors against the skyline and, with summer gone, the miniature streams had filled and the sound of running water mingled busily with the bleating of grazing sheep.

Adam was a good listener and as they followed the old coffin track which wound round the shoulder of

Chuff Tor then zig-zagged down to the Hollow he often surprised her with his knowledge of the moor's distinguishing marks until he reminded her that her cousin's letters had contained such good descriptions that he had no difficulty in recognition.

"There, for instance, is the spot where you slipped in the bog and didn't dare move till Hattie's son came to find you," he said, "and over there are the old tin workings where Sylvie found a dead ewe with its newborn lamb and carried it home. What happened to the lamb? She never told me."

"It died," she answered briefly, and was rather silent for a while. It was she and not Sylvie, of course, who had found and carried the lamb home — but she remembered uneasily that their personalities had sometimes tended to merge in the effort to remain as truthful as possible. It was a little disconcerting, she thought, how much he seemed to remember of things she herself had forgotten.

"What's changed your cousin?" he asked her suddenly as they started on the downward path to the Hollow.

"How do you mean?" she asked warily. "Sylvie's no different from when you first met her."

"On that occasion I had little opportunity for discovering anything beyond that conspicuous beauty, which was also a startling likeness," he replied humorously. "We hardly got around to exchanging life histories. I only meant that she seems to have lost interest in the things she used to write about with such fondness. It's difficult to imagine her running wild as you do."

"She never did," said Sarah, then added hastily: "I mean, she never ran wild in the sense of forgetting to be suitably clad or not doing her face, and lately — well, she's had other interests and I think she got a bit fed up with the moor." It sounded a lame enough explanation, she thought, regretting those rash outpourings to a stranger she had never expected to meet, but he seemed to accept it without much surprise.

"Young Bannister, I presume you mean, giving her a taste of more sophisticated pleasures," he said. "Well, it's natural enough, I suppose, to want excitement and a good time when you're as decorative as that, but it would be a pity if she allowed her head to be turned for the sake of a passing phase."

"Sylvie's head isn't easily turned," Sarah said with careful understatement. "She's quite accustomed to men falling for her, and can look after herself very well."

His smile was a little ambiguous, but he made no comment and presently she asked:

"Are you jealous of Nick?"

"Should I be?"

"I don't know. It would depend, I suppose, on how much you cared."

"Are you, by any chance, asking me my intentions?" he said, and she smiled, unabashed, knowing that although he was evidently not prepared to satisfy her curiosity, neither was he taking exception.

"Certainly not, that's Father's privilege," she replied rather primly, then spoilt the chance of putting him in his place by stumbling over a hidden rock and sitting down abruptly.

"Serves you right for trying to high-hat me," Adam said unfeelingly, but he reached down to pull her up and as she stood for a moment between his hands, he saw the merriment fade from her face.

"What's the matter? You didn't hurt yourself, did you?" he asked sharply.

Yes, dear Professor, she wanted to reply, *I've hurt myself beyond repair for lack of a little foresight ... how was I to know what I was laying up for myself when I wrote those letters?* Instead, she pulled away from him, brushed herself down, and replied coolly:

86

"Not at all, but *you* be careful, Adam. You could easily knock up that ankle again if you gave it a twist."

"So I could," he agreed, looking amused. "Is that what you're hoping for to gratify that passion for lame ducks?" He spoke teasingly because he had been aware of a most inexplicable desire to kiss her as she stood looking up at him with an expression he did not understand, but she answered him gravely as if he had asked her a serious question.

"I could never wish for something that would give you pain," she said. "My hope is always that you won't be hurt, or even disappointed — by anyone."

The deep lines about his mouth still retained their humour, but his eyes were gentle as he replied :

"That is a charming admission that you're not so indifferent to my feelings as you like to pretend. Were you trying to warn me that my affections might be in danger?"

"No, not exactly, but one can build up something for oneself that isn't there," she said carefully. "One can expect too much, perhaps. Anyway, let's get on and make our wishes — Granny will be so impressed by the tea that they're all bound to come true!"

No, he decided with relief as they made their way down to the Hollow, the young Sarah might not be entirely unscarred by life's injustices, but as yet she had only battled with the disappointments of a loveless childhood. He hoped sincerely that she would not again lay her heart at the feet of some man as unperceptive as her father. . . .

The Hollow proved to be a strip of stony wasteland sheltered from the weather by rocks and scrub. A gypsy caravan standing by the stream gave the place a picturesque air with its faded paint and yellow wheels, but the pile of used cans and bottles pushed underneath it was an unsightly reminder of probable squalor. A few hens scratched about amongst the scrub and a tethered goat, its udder swollen with milk, bleated peevishly as it sighted Willie.

"Hi, Granny! Can we try our luck at the pool?" Sarah called out. "My aunt has sent you a pound of your favourite tea in case you should feel like telling our fortunes."

A face peered through one of the caravan's dirty windows, then the door opened and its tenant stood at the top of the steps. Granny Coker was a remarkable figure by any standards, Adam thought, observing her with interest. She was enormously fat, her girth accentuated by the layers of indiscriminate garments which hung about her person, and she was certainly dirty. She could be any age and might have been handsome once before the many folds of flesh had blurred her features, Adam thought, catching a hint of coquetry in the appraising glance she gave him. Her gypsy origin betrayed itself in the darkness of eyes and skin, and the black hair, carelessly pinned and probably verminous, showed little trace of grey.

"Well now, if it isn't the l'il brown maid!" she said, her bright eyes darting avidly from one to the other of them. "'Tes a brave l'il while since you came visiting Granny — have you brought a fellow of your own at last to ask the piskies' blessing?"

"He's not a fellow in that sense," Sarah answered, evidently undisturbed by probably familiar personalities. "This is Professor — I mean Mr. Adam Soames who is staying with us."

"How do you do, Mrs. Coker?" Adam said, his lips twitching at the slip.

"Adam ..." said Granny ruminatively, her eyes running over him with lively interest. "That's a name spells promise of comfort and the fruits of the earth — not meaning they sour apples, neither. So you've come seeking Granny's good opinion, which is only proper ... let me look at your hand, good sir."

Adam held out his hand and she took it, running a dirty finger along the lines of the palm. Her touch was surprisingly delicate, he found, and though he submitted with amusement to the time-honoured opening gambit of the professional fortune-teller, he was not so unacquainted with strange happenings in other lands as to scoff.

"And now give me your'n, m'dear," she said to Sarah, and went over both hands, her lips moving soundlessly.

"Aye," she said then, lifting her eyes to Sarah's, "'tes all written here and no cause for 'e to doubt ... your gentleman's right for you, lover, and you for 'e, as I don't doubt 'e knows already."

Sarah's casualness vanished and she snatched her hand away, her cheeks suddenly scarlet.

"That proves what a fraud you are, Granny," she exclaimed, trying without much success to laugh. "The gentleman is a friend of my cousin's and it's she who should have brought him here, not me."

"Then why didn't her? Because she'd be feared what Granny might see, for all she makes fun of the Gift. Don't 'e let she take this one from 'e, lover, there's nought in her pretty hand matches up with his'n."

"Well, we'd better be getting back," Adam said, thinking it time to make a move before more random shots should add to Sarah's discomfort. It seemed plain that the queer old woman had a rough fondness for the younger of the cousins, but doubtless the less favoured of the two had proved a more fruitful subject.

"Yes, we should be going," she was saying now with considerable relief. "Well, goodbye, Granny, and thank you. Let's hope the piskies will make off with our offerings as a mark of goodwill. I could do with a change of luck."

"You'll have to pay us another visit to find out, won't 'e then? Come back tomorrow, lover, afore they changes their minds," the old woman said slyly, getting to her feet with some difficulty.

"Not tomorrow, it's my day for the spastics," Sarah said quickly, wondering why she felt reluctant to return.

"Then do you, sir, bring t'other young lady, 'tes all the same to the piskies if they've a mind to favour you. Besides, for all her laughs at Granny and calls the Gift a pack of nonsense, her'll be curious enough to see if her own siller's gone."

"What do you mean? Sylvie wouldn't come here on her own. She doesn't believe in the piskies."

"And that's why her siller's left at the bottom of the pool. Didn't you mind that new florin shining away in the sun? Here yesterday she were with that handsome young spark from the town who thought to fix the spell by insulting me with a pound note when they left."

"In that case the pixies — or their appointed agent — possibly hadn't time to oblige before we turned up today," Adam said quite pleasantly, but Sarah detected a new note in his voice and he was no longer smiling. "Come, Sarah, we must leave Mrs. Coker to get on with whatever chores we've interrupted."

Granny, too, evidently heard the change in his voice and for the first time there was a trace of the gypsy whine in her own as she began to wheedle.

"I meant no harm, giving t'other young lady away. She often comes here with that same fellow to park the car down the far end of the Hollow for a bit of a chat and a cuddle. A fine set up young chap, too, and his pockets well lined, which is pleasing to any young maid who likes a bit of fun, and no expense spared. There's all kinds of gentlemen, though. Now, I don't suppose you, sir, would make the mistake of slipping me a pound note?"

"No, I wouldn't," said Adam crisply, and politely raised his hat to her before shepherding Sarah down towards the stony track which had brought them down.

CHAPTER VI

THEY walked the rest of the way home, and just as they reached Slattery she said with rather forced brightness:

"It wasn't a very successful introduction to the piskie pool, was it, Professor? You'd better take Sylvie tomorrow to learn your fate. There's no telling, but her florin as well as yours may have disappeared."

"So all our wishes will come true and Granny the richer by four bob," he said, matching her effort with equal lightness. "I don't think, somehow, that I'd place such faith in the pixie's promises, and your cousin, I fancy, would much prefer a trip into town. Granny must wait till another day."

"That's courting trouble. Piskies are jealous and easily offended. They could well put a curse on your wishes if you slight them by not going back to find out," she said, and her eyes had grown so big and dark that he knew she half-believed what she was saying.

"Don't be absurd!" he exclaimed, and sounded impatient because for some reason she disturbed him. "If it's any consolation, I didn't wish for anything, so there's nothing to lose, is there?"

"But I did," she said unhappily, "and my wish was important to me. I don't suppose I'll get it if you cheated. Didn't you wish for *anything*, Adam?"

"Not a thing," he replied cheerfully.

They had paused in the porch to allow Sarah to kick off her muddy shoes before entering the house, and he became suddenly very much aware of her. Outside, although the sun had already dipped behind Ramstor, it was still late afternoon with long shadows thrown across the lawn, but here where the vine twisted its branches so thickly round portico and pillars, they were enclosed in a square of green dusk. Sarah was still looking at him with a mixture of reproach and disappointment; without her shoes she seemed very small and he reached out to her with a fond, protective gesture of which he was quite unconscious.

"Sarah ...?" he said on a soft note of enquiry.

He had spoken her name as a lover might and she responded instinctively, putting her hands in his, unaware of her own simple acceptance. He drew her close against him and although he did not kiss her there was no need. It was one of the moments of pure contentment that sometimes came to her out of the blue and she thought of the wish she had made at the pool and knew gratitude to the piskies ...

The front door was ajar and the rattle of a loaded teatray being carried across the hall broke the spell.

"What did you wish?" Adam asked, releasing her, but she shook her head at him.

"Don't you know you must never tell?" she said seriously. "Now, will you join the others in the parlour, Adam, while I sneak Willie through to the kitchen? I'm really supposed to take him round by the back because of Father's cats."

Sylvie had not returned when they reassembled again before dinner, and they were half-way through the meal when she telephoned to say that she would be late. She refused to say where she was ringing from and enquired pertly whether Adam was missing her.

"I shouldn't think so," Sarah replied with some tartness. "You haven't been over-generous with your company of late."

"So what? All the better for you! Is the crush developing nicely?"

"What's the matter with you? You sound a bit tight."

"I am a little. Nick says —"

"Are you with him?"

"Of course."

"Where?"

"Never you mind. Just tell Aunt Fran I'll be late back and kiss the Professor good-night for me if he shows signs of wilting in the family circle. Be seeing you. . . ."

She had rung off before Sarah could think up a withering reply, and she returned to the dining-room with a small nagging sense of disquiet. This, she supposed, was only another exercise calculated to bring the dilatory Adam up to scratch, but there had been a new note of recklessness in her cousin's voice and she remembered how persuasive Nick could be when he set out to charm, and Sylvie's own frank admissions that evening on the landing. Having delivered the message, she returned to her place at the table and sat scowling so fiercely at Adam that he raised an enquiring eyebrow.

"Am I in your bad books again, or is it Sylvie I've offended?" he asked with amusement.

"Neither," she said, looking away hurriedly. She had been unaware that she was scowling, a habit she had when something distressed her, but her aunt, familiar with this misleading sign of mental disturbance, said quietly:

"Let sleeping dogs lie, Sarah. People don't thank you for misplaced concern."

"What an odd remark. If Sarah shows concern for her cousin that's only as it should be, though I fancy that naughty puss knows what she's about, eh, Adam?" Gilbert said. He seemed to have forgotten his earlier complaints and perhaps, thought Frances a shade cynically, he had even convinced himself that such devious methods were bound to hasten a declaration.

"I wasn't, as it happens, referring to Sylvie," she said deliberately, and caught Adam's eye across the table. One eyebrow went up again, this time in mute enquiry, and Sarah rose from the table rather hurriedly.

"Talking of sleeping dogs, Willie hasn't had his dinner, so will you please excuse me?" she said, and bolted from the room.

Sylvie had forgotten her key or, perhaps, she had never intended to be so late home. She returned in the small hours of the morning and was obliged to throw pebbles at Sarah's window in order to get in without disturbing the household. Sarah, aroused from her first sleep, was anxious to return to her slumbers and catch up with the beginnings of a pleasant dream, but Sylvie seemed reluctant to go to her own room. While Sarah climbed back into bed she stood examining her face in the mirror by the light of the one hastily lit candle, then sat down on the dressing-table stool, evidently wanting to talk. She still communicated that thread of elation which Sarah had sensed over the telephone, and volunteered without being asked that she had spent the evening at Nick's flat in Tawstock.

"Was that wise?" Sarah asked, aware that something was required of her but unsure of the right response, and Sylvie replied glibly:

"It wouldn't be the first time. What's wrong about that?"

"Well, if a divorce is pending, doesn't one have to be careful?"

"Why? *He's* divorcing *her*."

"Yes, but don't people like the Queen's Proctor go snooping around?"

"So what? If I'm cited, Nick could do no less than marry me."

"That would shatter Father's illusions. He might turn a blind eye if Nick was the innocent party, but if you were cited he'd never get over it," Sarah said, and quite suddenly Sylvie was weeping.

"What do Uncle Gil's illusions matter? Is it my fault if he's stuck me up on a pedestal like one of his stupid pieces of china?" she wept, and Sarah was instantly wide awake.

"Sylvie, have you and Nick been lovers?" she asked, wondering why such a possibility had never occurred to her before.

"Of course! I wondered when the penny would drop. Why did you suppose we quarrel so much? We quarrelled again tonight over Adam because I pretended I liked him better ... now I've shocked you, I suppose — you wouldn't understand anything more adult than a safe schoolgirl crush ..." Sylvie suddenly flung herself across the bed and Sarah's arms, from long habit, closed round her. Even as she remembered that brief little moment of self-knowledge which had come to her in the strange green dusk of the porch, she made no effort to refute Sylvie's assumption. She had no wish to bring comfort by an exchange of confidences and said rather sharply:

"Are you only using Adam to make sure of Nick, then?"

"I'm never sure of Nick, and that's his attraction ... at least he's someone to fall back on if Nick shouldn't — oh, Sarah, help me!" It was a plea that had been made so often in the past that it probably meant no more than a bid for exoneration, but Sarah, for once, was unable to oblige.

"Would you really do that — take Adam if you can't have Nick?" she asked, gently withdrawing her embrace, and Sylvie sat up reluctantly. She looked exquisite and fragile in the candlelight with the tears, sparkling on her lashes and her parted lips still trembling and said rather like a cajoling child:

"Why not? At least he'd make an honest woman of me should the need arise — now I suppose I've shocked you!"

Sarah was profoundly shocked; not by the fact of a liaison which might or might not be true, but by the

95

willingness to make use of another man's regard should the matter become expedient. She thought of Adam's first love, so woefully confused with an image she herself had unwittingly helped to create, and every instinct in her cried out against such a wanton trifling.

"Has Adam ever spoken to you of Meg?" she asked abruptly, and saw the mockery in her cousin's face change to suspicion as she countered sharply: "Who the hell is she?"

"She's dead. They were once engaged to be married."

"Oh, is that all! Well, why, for heaven's sake, drag up some dreary old affair that's over and done with?"

"Because I'm not sure it is. It was Meg he saw in you the first time you met, and it's Meg he's hoping to find again, I think."

"What on earth wild fantasy have you dreamed up now?" Sylvie exclaimed, her face completely blank, and Sarah sighed. It had been rash, she supposed, to expect her cousin to understand an emotional disturbance which seemed perfectly logical to her, but having embarked on the subject she had to go on.

"Not fantasy —" she answered, "just one of those queer coincidences of resemblance that can come as a sudden shock. You and this Meg are apparently so much alike that Adam was knocked sideways."

"*Well*, of all the nerve!" Sylvie exclaimed. "Do you mean he only fell for me because I reminded him of some other girl? I don't believe it!"

"It's not so very hard to understand, surely. If you meet someone who seems so like your lost love, you must be half-way there already, I would think," Sarah said. "But be careful, Sylvie — Adam deserves better of you than to be used just to flatter your vanity."

"You and your images! When, might I ask, did you worm all this nonsense out of him — or have you just made it up to take me down a peg?"

"Of course not, neither have I done any worming. He

96

told me that wet afternoon when he came up to the stable-room."

They had been speaking in lowered voices to avoid disturbing the rest of the household, but Sylvie forgot in a renewal of chagrin and suspicion and exclaimed with sudden shrillness:

"I *knew* something had been going on! Don't think I can't see what you're after, pretending to avoid him, but sucking up to him on the quiet and probably making mischief as well to get a little second-hand attention."

"Do keep your voice down — you'll wake Aunt Fran. Nothing's been going on, so don't make such a thing of it," said Sarah, trying to keep her temper, but her face had whitened, throwing the tell-tale freckles into relief, and Sylvie knew she had scored a hit.

"It's you who are making a thing of it, my dear, dishing out warnings and advice like an elderly spinster crossed in love," she retorted. "Perhaps that's your trouble, poor prissy little cousin, but don't run away with the idea that taking that boring correspondence off my hands has given you the right to trespass on my preserves."

"It's given me the right to care whether he's hurt since I flatter myself I know the real Adam better than you do, so leave me to sort out my own troubles," Sarah snapped, thumping up her pillow to relieve her feelings, but as so often before at the height of some wrangle Sylvie's mood changed. The malice in her lovely eyes was replaced by curiosity and a hint of rueful apology and she said on a note of surprise:

"I believe you *are* in love with him, after all . . . no schoolgirl crush, but the real thing. Well, bad luck, darling, to fall in earnest for your make-believe hero, but don't kid yourself that I'll hand him over out of cousinly consideration. I'm not sharing any spoils, so I'm giving you fair warning."

"Oh, go to bed!" Sarah exclaimed, thoroughly exasperated, and flung herself back on the pillows. "I'm no hand at sharing spoils either, if it comes to that, so make your mind easy on that score."

"Oh, I'm not worried," Sylvie replied, yawning widely as she rose gracefully to her feet. "Still, it does make things more exciting to know that you want him too — or does that sound silly?"

"Very silly, so do shut up and go away. It's nearly three in the morning, so for goodness' sake let's get some sleep," Sarah said, then blew the candle out before her cousin could start another argument and pulled the bedclothes over her head.

The cousins did not meet until the next evening when Sylvie and Adam had returned from Plymouth. Whether or not Adam had derived as much pleasure as Sylvie from the city's entertainments he was certainly being rewarded with a flattering change of attitude. No one, thought Sarah with interest, could charm so convincingly as Sylvie when she set out to enslave, and Adam, if not precisely enslaved, must, nevertheless, be not a little encouraged by the first indications of capitulation. Gilbert, also aware of promising signs of submission in his capricious niece, allowed himself to expand almost paternally towards his guest; only Frances, sitting a little apart, spoke with her usual economy and observed them all with a watchful eye that was faintly satiric. Sarah, uncomfortably aware of her own failure to contribute gaily to the general mood of relaxed expectancy, made her excuses early and took Willie round the garden to sort out her uneasy impressions in private.

It was unfortunate that she should choose to slip into the house again by way of the forbidden front door, for one of the cats was scratching for admission outside the parlour and, before she could seize him, Willie had given chase. The resulting pandemonium brought everyone out into the hall; even Hattie emerged from the kitchen regions and joined in the shouting, while the cat, every white hair on end, shot like a ghostly apparition up the stairs and down again, pursued by the yelping dog.

"Shut the door! Shut the parlour door before they get in and break something valuable," shouted Gilbert, quite pale with rage. "Sarah, if you can't control that animal any better than you control your own limbs you must keep it in the stable — oh, for goodness' sake!" as Hattie hit out with a wet dishcloth and caught him smartly on the ear.

It was Adam who eventually seized the cat by the tail and threw it into the parlour and slammed the door while Jed at the same moment floored Willie in a flying tackle and hauled him off to the kitchen. Adam stood laughing helplessly while he dabbed at several scratches on his hand and Sarah, whose alarm had been occasioned by the inevitable effect on her father rather than fear for the animals' safety, subsided into nervous giggles.

"Really! I see nothing to laugh at!" Gilbert said huffily, addressing his ribald guest, then rounded on his daughter on whom he could relieve his feelings with greater freedom. But Sarah, for once, was unabashed by his caustic comments; the emotional disturbances of the past forty-eight hours had built up to a point where release of some sort had become essential and she could not stop laughing. Frances, giving her niece a shrewd glance, persuaded her brother back to the parlour where Sylvie had already retired to soothe the frightened cat, and when the door was firmly shut, Sarah found herself alone with a suddenly unamused Adam.

"Stop it," he said quietly.

"I c-can't . . ." she choked, and he slapped her sharply across the cheek.

"Why did you do that?" she asked staring up at him in bewilderment, but restored once again to sobriety.

"I'm sorry, but it was the best way to deal with
99

incipient hysteria," he said. "Funny though it was, that little pantomime hardly merited such unrestrained mirth. What's been upsetting you?"

"Nothing," she muttered, staring down at his shoes and wishing he would go away.

"That, of course, is the invariable answer when one's too stubborn to admit the truth. Was it your midnight quarrel with Sylvie?"

She looked up, thoroughly startled, and found he was watching her with a rather strange expression.

"Did you hear us, too?" she asked. "We weren't really quarrelling, you know."

"Weren't you? Your cousin seems to think you resented young Bannister's preference for her company last night. It always was Sylvie he was interested in, you know." He spoke so gently that she did not at once catch his meaning.

"But of course," she said. "One would have to be blind or half-witted not to realize that."

"And you, my stubborn Sarah, are anything but half-witted, so be sensible and adult before you get really hurt," he said, and touched the mark he had left on her cheek with tender apology.

She sprang away from him as if he had slapped her again, his meaning suddenly all too clear. How dare he offer advice, insult her with kindly warnings, when it was he who was responsible for her turmoil of mind?

"Did Sylvie imply that the plain little cousin had lost her heart and was consequently consumed with jealousy?" she asked him, rage mounting within her.

"Not in so many words, but she was concerned in case you had misinterpreted some of her remarks."

Yes, thought Sarah savagely, Sylvie would be good at dropping hints that could be taken several ways without committing her to anything specific.

"Things were said that had to be said, but nothing was misinterpreted, so mind your own business, Professor," she snapped back at him, and he smiled.

"When you address me like that it's always a sign that I've either trespassed or blundered," he said. "If I've trespassed it was with the best of intentions, and if I've blundered, I apologize."

"In that case, I accept your apology," she replied, trying to recapture some dignity, then stood shuffling her feet on the flags while she listened to the slow ticking of the grandfather clock in the corner and wished the growing silence between them did not seem so ominous.

"Thank you," he said at last, then reached out suddenly for her hands and pulled her towards him.

"Still turning your back on me? I wonder why," he said softly, but although she looked startled she did not draw away.

"Do I do that?" she asked, sounding chastened.

"You know you do. Just as soon as I flatter myself – I'm getting somewhere, you slam the door in my face and run away."

"Oh, no..." she said earnestly, all thoughts of her recent resentment forgotten. "Oh, no, dear Professor... if I slam the door it's because I must, but never, never think I've turned my back..."

The clock's ticking sounded loud in her ears, as loud as the quickened beat of her heart, then he said: "Sarah..." speaking her name with the same questing tenderness he had used that day when they had stood together in the leafy dusk of the vine-covered porch, and his fingers tightened round her wrists, drawing her closer just as he had then.

Whether he would have kissed her this time or not she never knew, for the parlour door opened suddenly and Sylvie stood there, the cat in her arms, both regarding them with the same wide, unblinking stare.

"Why on earth are you both still standing out here in the cold?" she asked. "Or am I by any chance being
101

tactless?" The smile she bestowed on Adam was mischievously enquiring, but her caressing fingers must have dug too hard into the soft white fur, for the cat spat and sprang out of her arms.

"Well —" said Sarah a little awkwardly, aware that after their nocturnal exchanges, there could be little pretence between them, "— I'll say good-night and go to bed. Thank you, Adam, for your deeds of valour — I hope you weren't badly scratched."

"I'm surprised you didn't take him down to the stable-room to bind up his wounds," Sylvie said, and looked quite surprised when Adam gently pushed her back into the parlour, saying good-humouredly: "We've had enough feline exhibitions for one evening, so compose yourself for a little soothing conversation before we all follow Sarah's example and seek our rest. Good-night, Sarah."

"Good-night," she replied, and when the door had finally closed behind them, ran first to the kitchen to comfort Willie before taking herself up to bed.

The weather turned cold the week of Goose Fair and an air of impending change seemed to touch their comings and goings at Slattery, as if the first frosts heralded more than the approach of winter. Sarah, looking forward to the great day with a renewal of excited anticipation, was still conscious of some flaw in her expectations as if the fair was to put a period to the familiar pattern of her childhood and nothing would ever be quite the same again. Sylvie, too, seemed to be aware of change, or perhaps she was only now realizing that Adam's departure was nearly upon them and she had tarried too long playing games which had merely delayed that desired declaration.

Sarah wondered if Adam would propose before he left or whether he was intending to leave her in doubt, hoping she would miss him. She could sense that in some measure he had been disappointed, but it was not easy to judge how much that mattered, and already he seemed to be slipping out of their lives, suggesting that he was no more than a transitory visitor obliged to them for pleasant hospitality but aware that it must come to an end. He drove into Cornwall several times to supervise preparations for the coming Survey and sometimes Sylvie went with him, but whether or not these expeditions proved fruitful in other respects, Sarah never knew. Since the night of their quarrel, the cousins had carefully avoided further intimacies and Sylvie was keeping her own counsel, while Sarah spent much time in the stable-room writing up her journal.

The day of Goose Fair arrived, and when Sarah went upstairs that evening to change out of her slacks she took more thought than usual as to what she would wear. The country girls coming from far and near for the traditional junketings probably saved up all the year to look their gayest and do credit to their young men, she knew, for to many of the isolated farmsteads, Goose Fair was the one social event in a long twelve months.

She chose a gay pleated skirt she had never worn because the variegated colours had seemed too bright, but as she twisted in front of the old-fashioned pierglass and watched the skirt spin round her with the merriment of a child's humming top, she felt suddenly a little reckless. She thrust her feet into scarlet sandals to match her sweater, knowing they would soon be ruined on the muddy fairground, and borrowed one of Sylvie's expensive head-scarves to tie over her hair.

They were to meet Nick at the hotel in the square to start the evening with the traditional goose dinner which every small restaurant and cafe in the town would be serving tonight, but they were late in starting, for Sylvie kept them waiting while she changed her dress yet again, and she looked none too pleased when Adam admired Sarah's new skirt and ignored her own attire.

103

Her ill-humour did not improve as Adam manoeuvred the car with some difficulty through the jostling crowds in the town, but Sarah was impervious to moods as she hung out of the rear window determined to miss nothing of the traditional gaieties. The cheapjack stalls set up on the pavements were doing brisk trade, hawkers dodged nimbly in and out of the slow-moving traffic peddling their wares, and a white glare in the sky marked the fairground up on the hill, music and the throb of the dynamos drifting down on the frosty October air.

Adam found a parking space for the Rover with some trouble and told the girls to go on to the hotel while he locked up the car. Sylvie eyed her cousin's gay, swinging skirt with grudging interest, then, observing how the bright scarf knotted under her chin lent her plain little face a curious piquancy, exclaimed indignantly:

"That's one of my best Jacqmar scarves you've pinched — what cheek!" The schoolgirl outburst did not accord well with the careful elegance of her clothes, and Sarah grinned.

"I didn't think you'd mind, you have so many. You might even let me keep this one — sort of blood money."

"For heaven's sake! What on earth's got into you tonight, and why should I give you my favourite Jacqmar?"

"Well, I *did* write those letters," Sarah said.

They were walking across the car park to the hotel and Sylvie hissed: "Shut up!" and glanced hastily over her shoulder, but Adam was some way behind them and she added quickly: "If you've ideas of making trouble for me on account of those silly letters you'd better think again. Adam's not likely to oblige you by transferring his affections, even if he believed your story."

"I shouldn't dream of telling him, it would hurt him too much to know you'd made a fool of him," Sarah

104

replied with a disconcerting absence of discomfort, and Sylvie frowned.

"Then don't make a fool of yourself, either, and take his compliments seriously," she snapped.

Sarah said nothing. On any other occasion she would have shrunk from such disregard for her more tender feelings, but tonight she was insulated in a bright bubble of expectancy and Sylvie's little shafts glanced off her. Even Nick, waiting for them impatiently in the bar, added to her sense of well-being, exerting his very considerable charm to draw her out and succeeding so well in making her feel herself desirable that she might have been in danger of losing her sense of proportion had she not become conscious of Adam's rather enigmatic regard from time to time.

When they had eaten their fill of vast helpings of goose and the traditional apple tart and scalded cream which followed, Nick proposed a civilized interim over brandy and cigars before tackling the hazards of the fair, but Sarah, whose enjoyment in her own surprising success had by now worn off, was impatient to get started on the real pleasures of the evening.

"If we don't go now, all the best prizes will have been won. Don't forget you said you were an ace at the rifle range, Professor, so I'm expecting to be showered with the spoils," she said, and he smiled across at her, remembering the afternoon when they had searched the moor for Willie and she had first stirred his interest. She had been a little fey, teasing some elusive memory in him that he could never quite pin down, and finally running away from him as if she, too, was conscious of disquiet. She was fey now, caught up in some heady dream of the movement, he thought, and was glad that she was still child enough to lose her new-found self-awareness in less sophisticated delights.

"If you and Sylvie would prefer to digest that gigantic

meal in civilized comfort before tackling the swings and roundabouts, you can follow us on later," he said to Nick as he obligingly got to his feet, but Nick, who appeared to be in an equally juvenile mood, pushed back his chair at once.

"Not on your life!" he laughed. "We'd never find you in all that crowd and I'm not risking losing either of my girls tonight. Come on, Sylvie — there's no need for running repairs to that enchanting face and the little cousin seems to manage very well without."

"The little cousin hadn't scorned the use of lipstick or a generous helping of my special scent to start the evening off, but perhaps you hadn't noticed," said Sylvie with some tartness, stuffing the compact back into her bag with none too good a grace.

"On the contrary, I noticed and was duly intrigued. Are you growing up, Sarah?"

He looked down at her with amused enquiry, his sleek golden head a little on one side, and for a moment Sarah experienced her old feeling of gaucheness in his company, conscious that Sylvie was annoyed and Adam was suddenly frowning. It had been very pleasant to be the centre of attention for once, but she was not at all sure that Nick wasn't above trailing a few red herrings to get his own back.

"I grew up a long time ago," she replied sedately. "The use of lipstick is no indication of suddenly acquired maturity."

"Which puts *me* in my place!" Nick said with a small grimace, but he took her arm possessively when they left the hotel to shepherd her through the crowds and it was not until they had threaded their way in and out of the cattle-trucks and horse-boxes jamming the market place that she was able to disengage herself. The pens were emptying now, for the main business of the day was done and people were making their way in a steady stream up the hill to the fair. Nick and Sylvie went on ahead, for Adam, whose ankle could still feel the strain of any steep ascent, had slackened his pace, and Sarah was glad to drop back with him. Nick was buying tickets at the turnstile while Sylvie impatiently scanned the faces of the couples that passed her.

"Come on!" she called impatiently when she saw them. "I thought you were just behind us. Have you been holding hands in dark alleyways on the way up?"

"No such luck — too many people about," Adam replied with a grin and for a moment she looked taken aback, then deciding that he had scarcely intended to be taken seriously, she slipped a hand through his arm and smiled up at him mischievously.

"You shouldn't make those sort of remarks in front of my little cousin. She's not used to polite gallantries and might misunderstand," she said, and although she spoke with a soft little air of cousinly concern, Sarah was well aware of the sting. Perhaps Adam hadn't heard in the general babel, she thought when he made no reply, but Nick had, and probably understood women too well to be deceived, for he observed casually:

"Then it's time the little cousin had a chance to try her wings, isn't it? I for one wouldn't say no to the intriguing possibilities of dark alleyways."

"Thanks for the compliment, but accustomed or not to polite gallantries, I'm selective in my choice of company," Sarah replied, recovering her composure, and he grinned appreciatively.

"You'll do, my pretty. What a pity I didn't discover your charms earlier, but it's never too late to begin, is it?" he said, his blue eyes bright with amused audacity, and she grinned back, aware with some surprise that in different circumstances she could have found a liking for him.

She turned to say something to Adam, but as the harsh glare of a roving spotlight caught him for a moment she surprised the face of a stranger. It was probably only a trick of lighting, but the skin seemed to be drawn so tightly over his bones that every line was deeply graven with a curious impression of angry bitterness. It was such a strange moment of revelation that she caught her breath sharply, then the beam of light passed on, and she knew it was only an illusion. Adam's face, if grave and unsmiling, was no longer the face of a stranger as he stood watching them both, and in the same moment Sylvie tugged at his arm impatiently demanding his attention.

"For goodness' sake, as we're here, let's go in and have our money's worth!" she scolded. "Haven't you and Sarah got a date to make yourselves dizzy on that ghastly roundabout?" But it was Nick, not Adam, who rode behind Sarah on a gilded, painted horse, supporting her with firm but exploratory hands as they spun round to the metallic blare of the canned music.

For a time they had all kept together, trying their luck at the various booths and exchanging greetings with acquaintances. Peavey village had turned out to a man, and Smales and Cokers and Dingles had converged in their confusing numbers to sink family differences in the traditional holiday. Sarah triumphantly demonstrated her skill at the coconut shies, but after that they had somehow become separated, and it was clearly a fruitless task to attempt to find one another again. Sarah, although bitterly disappointed at being cheated out of Adam's promised escort on the roundabout, soon forgot it in reliving the heady excitement of other years when Jed had been her companion of the evening and she a little girl with no more to trouble her than a scolding from Hattie for a torn dress.

"Another bob's worth," Nick kept shouting to the attendant when the music stopped and round they would go again. Sarah, a little drunk with the evening's surprises, and the nonsense Nick shouted into her ear as they were whirled around, up and down and ever faster, was conscious of nothing but the pure delight of a brief return to childhood. Nick was no more than a chance companion with whom to share her pleasure, and she rested against him with the same happy inconsequence with which she had once accepted the familiar support of Jed's hard young body.

CHAPTER VII

ADAM and Sylvie, having exhausted the fair's more inviting offerings, had found a small deserted tent in a corner of the fairground which was evidently a dumping place for empty beer crates. Adam, whose ankle was beginning to throb, suggested that they rested for a while and they sat on a couple of upturned crates and lit cigarettes.

Sylvie, who seldom smoked, soon threw hers away and began combing out her long hair which had become tangled in the wind. Adam watched her for a while, reminded again of that curious likeness to Meg. It was an impression rather than a likeness, he decided, conscious that he had been betrayed by an illusion created from dazzling fairness and delicate features, and the trick she had of tossing her hair back over her shoulders. Meg's eyes had been blue rather than violet and, strictly speaking, he supposed she had been pretty rather than beautiful. He reflected a little wryly that a student of psychology would doubtless have no difficulty in explaining the twists of a subconscious seeking the transference of an image, but it was no less galling to find oneself mistaken.

"What are you thinking?" Sylvie asked, and he smiled.

"Was I staring? I was only enjoying a very pretty spectacle. If that unromantic crate could turn into a rock you would do very well as a lorelei combing her hair and luring unfortunate sailors to their doom."

She liked the implication but was at a loss to follow it and said brightly: "Is that what they did? I thought they were plants."

"You're thinking of laurels, my lovely ignoramus.

Have you never heard the Rhineland legend of the maidens who sit on rocks combing their hair and singing so sweetly that no man can resist them?"

Sylvie looked interested. Adam quite often talked like Uncle Gil when he was trying to educate her literary taste which she found a great bore, but it seemed a promising start.

"Well, I can't sing, so I wouldn't stand much of a chance as a temptress, would I?" she said provocatively.

"You must know the answer to that one."

She lowered her lashes, then peeped up at him through them with a look that was as mature as it had been mischievously childlike a moment ago.

"You aren't very co-operative, are you, Adam?" she said. "Perhaps if I could sing to you you wouldn't find it so hard to resist."

"But then you see I'm not a sailor, so would surely be immune to your song," he replied immediately, and regretted his impulse to tease her as he saw the hurt surprise in her eyes.

"I don't understand you," she said, putting the comb away in her bag. "I thought — we all thought — but you've been with us for nearly a month and have only kissed me twice. It isn't as if you've had no chances, either."

"Chances I presumably share with young Bannister and, doubtless, several others," he countered indulgently, and she was not very flattered by the apparent absence of pique in his voice.

"Well, Nick at least knows what he wants and cares enough to be jealous," she said, and there was the threat of tears in her eyes.

"You really are very immature in many ways, Sylvie," he said, resisting the temptation to satisfy her demands and save further argument. "Because a man doesn't immediately declare himself, you take it as an affront. It's not a matter of running round the mulberry

111

bush to see who weakens first, you know. I thought you understood that it was only common sense to get better acquainted."

"Well, so we have. I'm not likely to know you any better than I do now!" she retorted impatiently.

"But you don't know me at all," he said humorously, and realized at once that he had merely confused her. It was not her fault that he had built up a false conception of her from letters which seemed to promise more than she had to give.

"I'm sorry if you've been disappointed in me," he said gently. "One is apt to read too much into letters when one is out of touch with reality. That was my reason for going back to the beginning."

The noise of the fair was an irritating reminder to Sylvie that she could have conducted this promising little interlude very much better if they had remained in the more civilized environment of the hotel. She wondered vaguely how Nick was getting on with Sarah and hoped boredom was paying him out for having chosen to pay her attention. It was not very nice to be obliged to Sarah for keeping Adam's interest alive, neither was it very nice to be obliged to the memory of a girl who was dead.

"Tell me about Meg," she said suddenly.

One eyebrow went up and he answered casually:

"Oh, has the little cousin been talking?"

"Was it a secret, then?"

"No, of course not. What do you want to know?"

"Sarah said I was like her. Why haven't you mentioned her before?"

"I didn't think you'd be interested in a past that is dead and done with."

"But you told Sarah, didn't you? She thinks you've confused me with a ghost, which isn't at all flattering."

"Does she? Well, there's a deal of perception in that young woman. Don't underrate her."

112

She eyed him warily, conscious that she might be on dangerous ground. She had not missed the distaste with which he had observed Nick's attentions during dinner, neither could she deny that the plain little cousin was showing a disquieting ability to hold her own in the matter of masculine interest. She had never had reason to doubt a loyalty which had always been taken for granted, but Sarah was in love, and in Sylvie's book, everything was fair in love or war.

"Do you find her attractive?" she asked him curiously, and his eyes twinkled at the naive surprise in her voice.

"Is that so hard to believe?" he answered, raising a quizzical eyebrow. "You rely too much on the advantages of a lovely face, my dear. Donne once wrote: 'Love built on beauty soon as beauty dies.' It's a salutary warning."

"Don who?" asked Sylvie sharply, searching her memory for the name of some discarded suitor who might have been rash enough to confide his disappointment to Sarah.

"John Donne — an Elizabethan poet, long since dead. You are surprisingly ill-read, considering your uncle's literary leanings," Adam replied a little wryly, and she fluttered her lashes at him.

"Oh, I never read," she said ingenuously. "Other people's opinions are such a bore. Anyway, what's the point of bringing up some fusty old poet who obviously can't have been with it to make that sort of silly statement?"

"No point at all," Adam agreed pleasantly, uncertain whether he wanted to laugh or slap her, and got to his feet. "Hadn't we better go and look for the other two?"

She stood up slowly, aware that she had somehow been found wanting, and suspecting that he probably never had intended to take advantage of this secluded refuge for more obvious reasons. Just for once the desire to subjugate was tempered by quite genuine humility and she reached up to touch his face with inviting fingers.

"Adam ..." she said softly, "are you really made of stone?"

He looked down into the exquisite face raised to his, and was both touched and troubled by the tears which were already trembling on her lashes. She had not, he knew, understood any part of his desire to rediscover a relationship which he might well have created for himself, but she was still very lovely and it would be churlish to refuse her.

"No, my dear, I'm very human, and you are more than kind," he said gently, and drew her to him, but even as he kissed her he found himself remembering how the young Sarah had lain against his breast for that brief moment in the dusky green of the porch at Slattery and been conscious of some strange, unspoken communication flowing between them. . . .

"There! You see what you can do when you really try," Sylvie said brightly as he released her, and he burst out laughing.

"Well, really!" she exclaimed, looking offended, and he patted her cheek solicitously, both relieved and slightly conscience-stricken that he felt no more than a passing regret for the loss of his dream.

"I'm sorry, but you sounded so like a bright little schoolmarm encouraging a backward pupil that I couldn't help laughing," he said. "Now, we really must go and hunt up the others or it will be too late to keep that date with Sarah."

The hour was growing late and the crowds were already beginning to thin out as they made their way back to the main attractions. Only a few screaming couples still patronized the roundabout and Sylvie said with rather childish satisfaction:

"You're too late for that date, Professor. It's pretty

decent of Nick, I must say, to have let himself in for this. He doesn't enjoy these sort of capers as a rule."

"Then he must have had a change of heart," Adam remarked with some dryness as Sarah, locked in Nick's arms, swung past them. She had not seen them and, indeed, thought Adam with an unexplained flash of anger, she was clearly unaware of her surroundings at all. The scarf had slipped back from her head, her eyes were closed, and her lips parted in a soft curve of pleasure. Every so often Nick brushed his chin across the short curls blown back by the wind of their passing and gave an absent tug to the gaily-coloured skirt as it billowed above her knees.

The speed was slackening now and as the revolutions of the horses grew slower and slower, Nick saw them both and waved. Sarah sat upright with a start and waved too, then called something over her shoulder to Nick who at once fetched a handful of coins from his pocket for another round.

"Oh, heavens! I'm going back to the hotel!" Sylvie exclaimed disgustedly, but she was quite unprepared for Adam's reaction. As the roundabout came to a stop he swung himself on to the platform and made straight for Sarah's mount.

"I think that's enough," he said very clearly. "Will you kindly get off, Sarah?"

Nick slid deftly over the horse's tail, looking amused, but Sarah still sat there and her expression was one of complete astonishment.

"I'll get off when I choose," she replied quite politely. "In fact I'll heap coals of fire upon your head and treat you to a ride which you don't deserve for having stood me up so rudely."

"You'll get off when I tell you, and that's here and now," he retorted, and her eyes widened.

"Why are you angry?" she enquired with mock-innocence. "Hasn't Sylvie been treating you nicely?"

115

"This isn't the place for childish recriminations," he said a little grimly, and before she had time to offer resistance, plucked her off the horse and set her on her feet with rough promptitude.

It was Nick who extended a hand to help her off the already revolving platform, then turned to murmur softly to Sylvie:

"Well, well ... the evening's full of surprises! Who'd have thought such a harmless frolic would have aroused the green-eyed monster in your well-disciplined suitor's breast?"

"Don't be absurd!" Sylvie snapped, watching her cousin disappear hastily into the nearest booth as Adam jumped off the roundabout. "He's simply annoyed at being kept hanging about when he's had enough for one evening."

"Well, you should know best whether he's had enough or not. I thought we were being rather tactful leaving the field clear for romantic dalliance in quiet corners. Wouldn't he play?"

"What are you getting at, Nick? I should have thought you'd made enough trouble for one night, without trying to stir up more."

"My exquisite creature, what *can* you mean?"

"You know very well. It wasn't kind to make a fool of Sarah just to score off me. She takes these things to heart."

"Does she now? I shouldn't be in such a hurry to voice your cousinly concern so often, if I were you, my pretty — it might put ideas into the wrong heads."

They were still standing in the muddy, trodden-down grass by the roundabout which was off again on its noisy gyrations. Adam must have followed Sarah into the booth, for there was no sign of him, and Sylvie, cold and disgruntled and aware of being found wanting for the second time that evening, felt an unfamiliar prick of alarm.

116

"You're not suggesting that *you've* been getting ideas, are you?" she said with a touch of scorn.

"No, no, I'm too hard a case to fall for a loving spirit, but your interesting Professor is a horse of a different colour. If you want him you'd better watch your step," he replied, and she looked angry.

"Thank you for nothing!" she snapped. "I thought you were so determined that he shouldn't cut you out. Have you changed your tune?"

"Oh, no, but I must be practical. If you still insist on marriage as the price of your favours, then the Professor's your man."

"When your divorce goes through, there's no reason why —"

He looked down at her, and the wry smile twisting his lips was repeated a little mockingly in his handsome eyes.

"My bone-headed charmer, there's every reason — alimony, the firm's prospects, to say nothing of the probability that you wouldn't want me once you'd got me," he said lightly.

"That's nonsense! You don't pay alimony if you're the injured party — anyway you've got plenty of money."

"That was the version you preferred to put about to fool your uncle. I have no grounds for divorcing Ruth."

"Then let her divorce you. If Uncle Gil thinks we've been lovers he'll hardly forbid the banns."

"No, no, my lovely, that cock won't fight. You stood out for all or nothing — remember?"

"I told Sarah we were."

"What on earth for? Just to rub her nose in it? Really, my love, you'd say anything to prove how irresistible you are. You'll be inventing a little stranger on the way next, if you think it will get you what you want."

"That's a filthy thing to say!" she exclaimed, her eyes filling. "Let Ruth divorce you as you planned at the

117

beginning. If she cites me Uncle Gil will just have to lump it."

His eyes were admiring, but that wry little smile still twisted his lips as he absently brushed off a sticky, persistent child demanding sixpence for the roundabout.

"But desire wanes with a surfeit of coy provocation and I'm afraid I don't think you're worth the risk of Ruth taking her capital out of the firm and leaving Bannisters to stew," he drawled. "Anyway, let's get out of here. We can settle our affairs more comfortably back at the hotel."

He put a hand under her elbow and began walking her towards the nearest exit. She was too used to his deliberate provocations to quarrel to pay much heed to his meaning, and was only conscious that the evening had been a hideous failure and she a fool to lend herself to such unrewarding junketings.

"Shouldn't we wait for the others?" she enquired rather vaguely, wondering without much interest, whether Sarah, too, was being subjected to a taste of plain speaking, but Nick gave her a pinch that was none too gentle.

"Don't be a spoil-sport, and take a word of warning from the wise. Have a care your second string doesn't tire of pursuing a beautiful mirage and settle for something more within reach."

"What do you mean, a mirage?" she demanded, her suspicions instantly aroused.

Even Nick had not been allowed to share the amusing secret of the letters, but it would not be surprising if such unaccustomed attention had gone to Sarah's head and she had admitted the truth when whirling around in that dizzy fashion with an escort who was all too skilled in extracting confidences.

"Nothing very profound, but a man needs more than the remnants of a beautiful dream to warm his bed," Nick replied, giving her another pinch, and at once they were plunged into one of their numerous quarrels.

They were outside the gates by then and were faced with an unpleasant walk back to town, for it had started to rain. Their abusive exchanges and recriminations were so familiar that neither of them took much hurt, and for Sylvie it was a distinct relief. Their wranglings passed unnoticed by the voluble stragglers accompanying them down the hill, for much beer and cider had been drunk and there was a deal of convivial singing and shouted boasts of sales and bargains effected earlier in the day, but Peavey villagers with sharper noses for local gossip nudged one another and winked knowingly. That young madam up to Slattery do be getting more than she bargained for, with her dilly-dallying, they told each other; didn't seem as if the tall stranger from foreign parts was coming up to scratch, for all the talk there'd been of love letters coming and going as regular clockwork . . .

For Sarah, following down the hill with Adam rather later, reaction had begun to set in. When Adam had whipped her so suddenly off her wooden charger she had felt no more than surprise, but as she glimpsed his face before Nick had handed her off the platform rather more politely, she caught her breath on a little gasp. Just so had his face looked earlier, trapped for a moment in the moving spotlight when Nick had been talking all that nonsense just to score off Sylvie. Then Sarah had thought that unconscious betrayal had been occasioned by her cousin's devious provocations, but now she remembered that it was Nick he had been staring at just as he had stared at them both on the merry-go-round before the music stopped, and it was she herself who had been the subject of gallant jokes concerning missed opportunities in dark alleyways. Was it possible, she thought, as she instinctively made her escape, that she could have aroused an emotion in Adam which all Sylvie's practised skirmishings could

119

not? Anything was possible at Goosey Fair, she told herself, still caught up in that light-headed state of unreality which had cushioned her all the evening, but when Adam strode into the booth after her and demanded to know in no uncertain terms why she felt impelled to make a spectacle of herself, she was not so sure.

"What on earth's the matter with you, Professor? There's nothing very outrageous about riding on a merry-go-round. You were going to do it yourself, if you remember, only you had other fish to fry," she said, possibly influenced by the fact that her random refuge had proved to be a fish-and-chip stall and the smell of frying was very pervasive.

"That's no concern of yours and don't call me Professor. This isn't a laughing matter," he snapped back with such an unfamiliar absence of humour that her mouth opened in a round O of astonishment.

"Well, really, Adam! I can't see why you've worked yourself into such a state," she said, trying to sound reasonable. "I was very disappointed, as it happens, that you ran out on our date, but I quite understand in the circumstances."

"What circumstances?"

"Oh, *honestly!* It was obvious that you would prefer to pair off with Sylvie, since if it wasn't for her you wouldn't be here at all, but I don't see why I should have to forgo my bit of fun on that account."

It was, she realized almost at once, an unfortunate, if innocent enough remark to have made in his present mood, for those asymmetrical eyebrows drew together in a dark, ragged line across the impressive nose and he succeeded in looking as if violence might be expected of him at any minute.

"If you wanted a bit of fun you shouldn't have chosen such a public spot as a floodlit roundabout," he retorted, and she bit her lip, trying not to laugh. He must have seen a betraying quiver, for he added more quietly: "Very well, so I'm making a fool of myself, but I've had about enough of female antics for one evening."

She sighed, remembering Sylvie's earlier petulance, and asked tentatively:

"Was Sylvie unco-operative? She can be very tantalizing, I know, when she likes to keep one guessing."

"Sylvie was more than co-operative, if you mean what I think you mean, so don't run away with the idea that I'm suffering from sour grapes. It's *your* behaviour I find hard to stomach. Borrowing a leaf from your cousin's book doesn't suit you at all."

Somebody jostled her, spilling chips down her skirt, and she was knocked against Adam who put a hand out to steady her. She was so close to him now that she could sense another emotion behind his anger.

" 'I didn't do it to annoy because I know it teases,' " she misquoted softly. "Nick just stood in for you; I don't suppose it gave him much satisfaction. Adam, were you jealous?"

"Would it please you to know that I was?" he evaded, at the same time taking out his handkerchief to deal with the greasy marks on her skirt.

"It would surprise me," she said, looking down at his bowed head and discovering with fondness a few white hairs in the nape of his neck, "but it's been rather a surprising evening altogether."

"Has it? Well, I won't surprise you any further with unconsidered answers to rash questions."

"I haven't asked any rash questions," she said sedately. "Do you know you've got four — no, five white hairs on the back of your neck?"

"Very likely, considering my advancing age," he replied, straightening up again, but the twinkle was back in his eye. "What about some fish and chips to cheer us up, since we're here?"

If it was a peace offering or merely an excuse to end the absurd disagreement, it worked very well. It was not possible, Sarah thought, to quarrel with any dignity when clutching newspapers precariously filled with oily offerings that tended to escape down one's bosom if not carefully controlled. Adam, she was delighted to find, was as adept at this manner of eating as she was and she wondered whether Sylvie and Nick were already back in the hotel and enjoying the more rarefied appetizers of Martinis and canapés while they waited.

Perhaps it was the rain which began to damp her ardour as they walked down the hill together, or perhaps, listening to the sounds of the fair receding behind them, it was the knowledge that she was no longer a child to look forward with untroubled anticipation to next time. Goosey was over and done with for another year and it was dispiriting to ponder on the changes that year might bring about.

"You're very quiet all of a sudden. Are you tired?" Adam asked out of a long silence between them.

"No. I was wondering where we'd all be this time next year and wishing Goosey could always stay the same," she answered, and he frowned in the darkness.

"Sarah . . ." he said with careful dispassionateness, "I hope you haven't placed too much reliance on young Bannister's behaviour this evening."

"What do you mean by behaviour? We didn't shout and sing or throw bottles about, even though you did seem to think riding on a roundabout was making a spectacle of oneself."

"Now, don't put out those prickles at once. I didn't mean anything of the kind. I was alluding to his rather marked attentions. I wouldn't like you to get wrong ideas about a young man who was possibly using you for his own ends."

"If," said Sarah, her temper rising, "you're going to model yourself on Sylvie and show an unnecessary concern for my tender feelings, you can save your breath. Anyone would thing I was a sort of half-wit to hear you both talk."

"Anything but a half-wit, my prickly little hedgehog, as I've told you before, but not, perhaps, very experienced," he replied pacifically, but she missed the fond inflection in his voice and was not appeased.

"And don't be patronizing," she snapped back. "You don't know me well enough to use the possessive tense *or* to call me a hedgehog."

They had come to the little cul-de-sacs and alleyways above the town, dark now and quite deserted, for they were almost the last of the home-going stragglers. Adam stopped and suddenly swung her round to face him in the shelter of an overhanging porch, remembering a little wryly the banter which earlier had stemmed from mention of these same dark alleyways.

"I know you better than you think, and there are times when I would dearly like to shake some sense into you," he said, and might have done so there and then had he not seen the strange expression in her eyes and kissed her instead. He knew he had been clumsy with his well-intentioned warnings, and was not surprised that she had reacted with such a prompt return to the prickly child of his first acquaintance, but there was nothing childlike in the way she had looked at him just then, and whether or not she had already lost her foolish heart to Sylvie's philandering young man, she made no resistance to his own demands.

For Sarah the moment was only a rich completion of the evening's magic. She did not think it strange that anger should turn so swiftly to something different, for she was used to such inexplicable changes in herself, neither did she question her own rectitude, for was it not she who had kept Sylvie's image green?

"Well, now," Adam said softly as she lifted her face once again in blind invitation, "after this you can hardly shut me out with prim withdrawals into that private world of yours ... you're very lovable, Sarah ... very lovable and far too trusting...."

"I don't think so... I've known about you for a very long time ... though not perhaps as much as you've known about me," she replied dreamily, and he was aware again of that elusive little spark of recognition that frequently teased him. Her eyes were closed and he thought she probably spoke from a self-induced state of make-believe, fostered by the events of the evening, and felt a little disturbed.

"How can I have known so much about you on such short acquaintance?" he asked her gently, and her eyes flew open, then immediately avoided his. She looked so like a little girl caught out in some careless slip of the tongue that he had to smile, but almost at once, Sylvie's warnings returned to trouble him. He had given way to an impulse which had nothing to do with any desire for casual dalliance, but if young Bannister was, as he suspected, responsible for this dangerously receptive mood in her, he had no right to take unfair advantage.

"I think we're both a little drunk with the local high jinks, and you, my child, are probably still dizzy from all those joy rides on the roundabout," he said lightly before she could answer his question, and she backed away from him as if he had suddenly slapped her.

"What you're trying to say is 'Don't be such a naive little fool, Sarah, as to take me seriously.' Well, I won't, so you needn't look at me with that insulting air of indulgence," she said, and she looked so endearing with her short hair clinging in flat, wet curls to her head, and the freckles standing out on her suddenly angry face, that he had to resist very firmly a temptation to take her back into his arms.

"Nothing of the sort," he said, aware a little wryly that he seemed fated to tread clumsily when he desired nothing more than her well-being. "What I was trying to

124

say was it's easy to misunderstand a mood which because of certain unexpected circumstances takes on a false air of truth. Things said and promises made on such occasions which, though possibly quite sincere at the time, can prove embarrassing in the cold light of morning."

"I made no promises that I can think of, but if anything I've said is going to embarrass you, Professor, then I take it all back. It was Nick, after all, who drew your attention to the profitable uses of dark alleyways, so I took it for granted that you wouldn't waste your opportunities on the way down," she said, and would have ducked under his arm and escaped if he hadn't firmly pressed her back into the porch, now as angry as she.

"How dare you credit me with such vulgar motives?" he rapped out at her. "I admit that my behaviour might well have been mistaken for the casual philanderings of your less discriminating friend, but I can assure you I'm not given to forcing my attentions on reluctant young women for the fun of it — neither, if I may say so, were you noticeably reluctant."

"Well, and what did you expect? Didn't Nick say in front of you all that it was time the little cousin learnt to try her wings? It would have been all the same had he walked me back instead of you and possibly a lot more instructive."

He was too angry, and surprisingly, too hurt to recognize bravado in this last childish taunt and retorted acidly:

"Very likely. I don't doubt that the knowledgeable Mr. Bannister would be delighted to be called upon for a course of instruction in the art of making love, but I don't advise you to try it. You're not cut out for the sort of casual affair your cousin would doubtless take in her stride."

For a moment Sarah's own rage cooled sufficiently for

125

her to say with some surprise:

"You sound as if you wouldn't mind very much if Sylvie *did* have affairs. Is that the modern approach to a successful courtship, or am I just being naive?"

"You are, I fancy, being deliberately naive, not to say foolhardy," he replied, trying to control himself. "Do I strike you as the sort of man who'd be content to turn a blind eye so long as he got what he wanted?"

"No, you don't. On the other hand, you don't strike me as a man who's very much in love, either, if you don't mind me saying so."

"I mind very much, since it's none of your business. Don't measure other people by the sentiments you imagine you feel for young Bannister. One learns in time to dismiss calf-love with other adolescent conceptions of romantic behaviour."

"*Calf*-love! Is that what you think I'm suffering from?"

"Well, perhaps that was a little unkind. Calf-love, puppy-love — whatever one likes to label the first stirrings of sex can be just as painful as a more mature involvement and a lot more confusing," he said, but although he spoke with greater tolerance, he could not quite keep the bite out of his voice.

"And you think because I wasn't — noticeably reluctant I think you said — that I was using you as a kind of substitute?" She shivered as she spoke, feeling a cold little trickle of raindrops run from the ends of her hair down the back of her neck.

"Not consciously, perhaps, but it was a very natural reaction, I expect. I would have liked to think that I could claim a small part of your indulgence for myself, but that, no doubt, is being egotistical."

"It is indeed, Professor, since you were clearly doing the same thing yourself and using me as a stand-in for Sylvie. Men want it all ways, don't they? I may be the plain little cousin who doesn't stand a chance with

126

Sylvie's besotted suitors, but I'm hanged if I'll oblige you both to make up for your disappointments."

"Is that how you think of my regrettable lapse?"

"What else should I think? I'm tired of being the stooge in Sylvie's affairs. If you want her, why in hell don't you muscle in and cut Nick out?"

"So that he might then fall back on you?"

"Oh, don't be ridiculous! He might show interest for a while to get his own back, but I'm not his cup of tea at all."

"No, you're not, or he yours, but I suppose it's no use telling you that. Catching someone on the rebound is quite a common occurrence, but not the right sort of happy ending for you."

"Why should you care?"

"Heaven knows! Perhaps because I've always had the feeling that we could have been friends if it wasn't for Sylvie and your own cock-eyed stubbornness. Now let's forget this unfortunate little episode. If it's any comfort to you, my sensibilities have most likely suffered rather more than yours, so chalk that one up to your credit."

"What do you mean?"

"Never mind. Just remember that whatever your private opinion of my well-meant interference, you can always treat me as a kind of inanimate safety-valve if you want to blow off steam, but I'm hoping the temporary loss of your heart is no more than a mild disorder."

She was overwhelmed with such blank astonishment that for a moment she was speechless. Could he really think that she would have responded so ardently to a man who meant nothing to her, or had his pursuit of Sylvie reached a point which rendered him blind to any emotions but his own?

"You see what you want to see, Adam — perhaps we all do," she said then a little helplessly, and shivered again.

"No, my dear. I see what my instinct rejects but my intelligence must accept," he replied gravely, and she suddenly stamped her foot.

"Oh, you're so stupid with your neat little conclusions and avuncular platitudes! You're so stupid, I could *spit*!" she shouted at him, and ducking under his arm, ran out into the rain and sped down the dark, deserted street.

It seemed to Frances Deverell that the night of the fair marked a turning point in Slattery affairs, although in what measure it was hard to define. Gilbert had gone to his room early complaining of the start of a cold and she had followed shortly, glad of the excuse for an extra long read in bed. The Tawstock party must have become separated, for she heard the two girls being dropped at the gate by Nick and much later, the sound of the garage doors closing on Adam's Rover followed presently by his quiet footsteps passing her door.

There was nothing in Adam's manner during the days that followed to suggest that anything was amiss, but if Sylvie was unusually malleable and attentive to his needs, Sarah was off-hand to the point of rudeness. Gilbert, never gifted for much perception, and made irritable by his cold which had resisted all attempts to stay its course, unwisely protested.

"Really, my dear! Do you have to behave with such boorishness to our guest?" he said when Adam was out of earshot. "You're hardly endearing yourself to your future cousin, which is a mistake, don't you think?"

"What do you mean, my future cousin?" Sarah said, and her aunt saw her face suddenly whiten as she spun round to face her father.

"Don't anticipate," Frances said smoothly. "Your father is being a little premature, I fancy."

"Scarcely without reason," her brother observed huffily. "In my day a young man who paid attention to a girl and accepted the hospitality of the family would have been asked his intentions long ago."

"I daresay, but times have changed. It would be extremely embarrassing to a casual visitor if he was expected to repay hospitality with a declaration," Frances said with a touch of humour.

"What on earth's got into you, Fran?" her brother asked impatiently. "Hasn't it been obvious from the start — that first meeting — all those letters?"

"Yes, well ... it was Sylvie herself who put such romantic ideas into our heads, if you think back. She's never been able to resist dramatizing her conquests."

"Talking of letters," Sarah broke in rather hurriedly, "someone's been in the stable-room snooping about among my papers."

"You aren't trying to suggest that you have a secret store of love-letters up there, I hope?" Gilbert, annoyed at being side-tracked from a more promising subject, spoke more unkindly than he meant, and Sarah flushed.

"My journal's there. No one's allowed to read my journal," she replied coldly, and her father gave a little snort of impatience.

"Oh, really, my dear child, have a little common sense!" he exclaimed. "Who on earth would want to wade through your girlish effusions? Diaries are notoriously egotistical and dull."

"Yes, Father, very likely, but my thoughts are private and one's privacy should be respected. Sometimes it's all one has," Sarah replied, and slammed out of the room, upsetting a pile of periodicals as she went.

"Now what on earth can she have meant by that remark?" Gilbert said, too astonished to comment with his customary tartness on his daughter's clumsiness.

"Perhaps she was simply speaking the truth. Sarah's learnt to value privacy," Frances replied, stooping to pick up the scattered magazines.

"Well, upon my soul, I don't know what's got into

everybody since that wretched fair!" her brother grumbled, blowing his nose with some violence. "Hattie's as cross as two sticks, you come out with extraordinary statements and Sarah seems determined to make the worst of herself. At least Sylvie has come to her senses and has stopped using her admirer from the garage to get a rise out of Adam."

"Let's hope she hasn't left it too long for her own comfort," Frances said. "It's a little late in the day to start rebuilding an image."

"What image, for heaven's sake?"

"The image which Adam presumably carried with him all those months — something rare and perfect — like one of your special pieces of porcelain."

"Which, indeed our Sylvie is. What's wrong with cherishing an image and coming back to find it real?"

"Nothing wrong, but sometimes unwise. Images can break."

"Very profound but distinctly far-fetched," Gilbert retorted with the old sarcastic intolerance. "You're forgetting, I fancy, the less rarefied link of that correspondence."

"No, I wasn't forgetting. It's the one aspect of this affair I fail to understand," she answered absently, then went on before he could comment: "I hope Sylvie *hasn't* been dipping into Sarah's journal. She mightn't mean any harm, but it's not a moment when Sarah will take kindly to having her private emotions exposed."

"Private poppycock! You'll be telling me next that the child imagines she's in love!"

"I think she is. I'm afraid she's in love with Adam. Does that surprise you?" Frances did not wait for his reply but went out of the room, quietly closing the door behind her.

Sarah, after that awkward little passage of arms with her father, had gone out on to the moor with Willie to cool her temper. The rain which had driven the merry-

130

makers home early on the night of the fair was the forerunner of the first of the autumn fogs and which could blanket the countryside for days on end, and already pockets of mist had formed in the hollows and were spreading across the moor gathering the rising damp from heather and bracken into wraith-like swirling folds. Every so often the mist would part to reveal the shape of a tor, a ragged line of broken stone wall, or a little group of ponies, huddled together. By evening it would be really thick. Sarah kept to the sheep-tracks knowing how easy it was to miss one's way by cutting through scrub and boulders, and tried to wrestle with her unquiet spirit.

She had been so engrossed in her thoughts and speculations that she had failed to notice Willie was no longer with her. She called and whistled, but to no avail, and although she strained her ears to catch any sound that might indicate that the dog was hunting, only the infinitesimal pops of dripping moisture and the distant cry of a bird broke the stillness. Willie had vanished into the mist like a wraith and Sarah was touched by her old fear. Reason told her that the farmer, Rowe, was unlikely to be out with a gun in this sort of weather, but alone in an eerie solitude where sound and vision alike were muffled and distorted, it was not difficult to allow fear to border on panic. Sarah stumbed among the rocks and undergrowth, shouting and waiting, shouting and waiting, her lips too dry to produce any more than the ghost of a whistle. She had the sense not to move far off the beaten tracks and when presently she found herself on the shoulder of moor which looked down on Slattery, and saw the house rising from the mist, her fears abated. It was only early afternoon now, so it was clearly sensible to return home and trust to the dog's intelligence to come back when he had exhausted both his curiosity and himself.

She could not find Jed, and Hattie when asked if by

any chance the wanderer had already made for home, answered impatiently and advised her not to go plaguing her family with foolish speculations.

"For they do be niggled by this pesky weather, and you dad in no mood for patience, what with his cold and one of his pet pieces broke," she said, and Sarah was momentarily diverted from her own trouble by a calamity which could have disastrous repercussions.

"Oh, *no!*" she exclaimed. "Which piece, and how did it happen?"

"One of a pair of they pesky li'l ole Dresden figures. Sylvie broke it."

"What a mercy! If it had been any of us we'd never have heard the end of it."

"Even Sylvie didn't get off without being called a meddling clumsy fool, for the first time in her life, I'll warrant," said Hattie dryly. "She'm upstairs in the stable-room sulking, so you'd best mind your step."

This information was quite sufficient to turn Sarah's thoughts for the time being. It had always been tacitly understood between them that the stable-room was hers and not to be shared without invitation. It seemed only too likely that her suspicions of the morning were right, and she ran across the yard and up the wooden steps to find out for herself.

Sylvie was sprawled in the chair with the broken spring, engrossed in the untidy pile of typescript on her lap. She looked up as Sarah burst into the room and went a little pink, but made no effort to hide what she was doing.

"I *knew* someone had been snooping — the papers were out of order. How dare you come up here behind my back and poke about among my things?" Sarah said, snatching at the journal which parted from its flimsy moorings and cascaded over the room.

"I was looking for something that belongs to me, as it happens," Sylvie replied coolly. "What are you in such a tizzy about — those lovelorn allusions to your dear Professor?"

"There's nothing of yours up here, so why pretend?" Sarah said, going on her knees to salvage the scattered pages of her journal.

"Oh, yes there is — Adam's letters. You said you'd kept them."

"They were written to me."

"Oh, come off it, love, the joke's over!"

"It was no joke to me. I deputized for you in the first place, but you lost interest long ago. You never bothered to read what I wrote or even the replies. Whatever misapprehension Adam laboured under, those letters were meant for me."

"Oh, now you're carrying your fantasy too far! Whatever kicks you got out of an imaginary love-affair with a stranger, you can hardly kid yourself that it was Sarah Deverell he was replying to."

"You wouldn't understand. He may have thought he was answering your letters, but it was me — my own personality — that inspired the replies. Why should you grudge me that?"

"Oh, come now, darling, if you go on like this you'll have me thinking you mean to make capital out of the wretched things. Hand them over — it's only common sense for me to run through them and have some clue to what I am supposed to have said!"

"No," said Sarah, sitting back on her heels, "you'll have to wriggle out of that one yourself. I won't use them in any way that can hurt you, but I won't give them up."

"That's silly! How can someone else's love-letters give you any satisfaction?"

"They aren't love-letters — not in your sense of the word."

"What other sense is there, for heaven's sake?"

"You wouldn't understand. Letters can be full of love

133

without using a single sentimental phrase."

"I think you must be crazy!" Sylvie exclaimed. "I suppose the truth is you've just invented something that isn't there to make up for your disappointment. Those early efforts were dull enough in all conscience — just like a running commentary, or a dreary documentary about mineralogy."

"He loves his work and the queer places it takes him to, and I found it interesting. That, you see, is one kind of love — there are so many. If you mean to marry Adam you had better try to understand what's important to him."

"Meaning you think you do?"

"Well perhaps I can't help knowing him better than you do, just as, of course, he knows more about me than I care for in the circumstances."

Sylvie's eyes narrowed. "So you *have* been having a little fun on the quiet, the two of you! I thought as much!"

"Oh, Sylvie, you're so naive!" Sarah exclaimed, uncertain whether she felt like laughing or crying. "You don't get to know a person simply by jumping into bed with them. I would think it was more than possible to enjoy making love without any conception of what the other person was really like. Do you know Nick — really know him, I mean?"

There was a small silence between them as if Sylvie was thinking and for once was endeavouring to be honest with herself. Then she said slowly: "No, I suppose I don't. He's going back to his wife," and quite suddenly she was weeping.

"D-don't you care?" she demanded resentfully when Sarah did not speak, and she moved uneasily.

"Of course I care, but how much do you?" she said gently. Sylvie, who possessed the mysterious art of turning tears off as quickly as she could turn them on, lifted a suddenly smiling face and said brightly:

"Not as much as you do, poor lovesick Sarah. I'm not the girl to sink into a decline for any man when there are so many good fish in the sea. Nick was an exciting experience which I don't regret, but Adam will do just as well."

Sarah had been conscious of a man's step on the outside stairway while Sylvie was speaking and presumed that it was Jed coming up for news of Willie. But it was Adam who, having knocked and been bidden to enter, stood in the doorway and said with interest:

"In what way will I do just as well?"

CHAPTER VIII

SARAH, wondering how much more he might have heard before opening the door, felt herself going scarlet, but Sylvie did not even change colour and stretched out an airy hand in greeting.

"Hullo!" she said, smiling up at him. "I was saying that you were probably a more suitable person to give an opinion on the age of Dartmoor than me. We were discussing Sarah's journal."

His regard went to Sarah's embarrassed face, then to the crumpled papers in her lap, and one eyebrow rose.

"It looks a little the worse for wear," he remarked. "Shall I put the pages in order for you, Sarah?"

"No!" she said ungraciously, and jumped up, but in her haste she dislodged a few more pages which fluttered to the ground at Adam's feet, and Sylvie laughed.

"She's afraid you might read things you aren't meant to see," she said mischievously. "There are some rather revealing passages relating to yourself, Professor."

"Really? I've always understood a diary is private," Adam said, stooping to retrieve the fallen pages and handing them back to Sarah, and Sylvie had the grace to blush.

"Oh, of course, and I wouldn't dream of snooping, but sometimes Sarah reads me bits, just for a giggle," she said, and failed to understand why her tactful explanation should cause such a change of expression in his face.

"The revealing passages concerning myself being the bits for your mutual amusement, I must presume," he said, and Sarah, meeting the sudden chilling eye of a stranger, cried out in protest.

"That's not true and you know it, Sylvie! I found you up here reading my journal, so why pretend?"

"You know why I was here, darling. I was looking for Adam's letters which you'd pinched, so you needn't accuse *me* of snooping." Sylvie said, adding hastily to Adam as she caught his sudden interested eye, "Don't think I'm suggesting my naughty cousin took a peek at your letters, Adam — she's only hidden them somewhere just to tease me."

"I shouldn't have thought you would have found them worth keeping."

"But of *course*! Haven't you kept mine?"

"No," said Adam with very definite finality. "Now, since I seem to have intruded at a not very propitious moment, I'd better take myself off again."

"I'll come with you," Sylvie said, throwing a triumphant glance at Sarah as she sprang out of the chair and caught up with him at the door. "Don't be cross, Adam, I was only teasing. As a matter of fact, I'm feeling pretty low. I've broken one of Uncle Gil's best Dresden pieces and he hasn't been at all nice about it, so do come up to the house with me and soothe him down."

Sarah, watching the hardness go out of Adam's face as he looked down at Sylvie clinging to his arm, wanted to throw something hard and heavy at them both. While she could find it in her heart to hate her cousin at that moment, she could still admire and envy the adroitness with which she was able to wriggle out of situations. What conclusion Adam might have drawn from those regrettable exchanges she had no means of guessing, but the look he gave her before following her cousin down the steps was disconcerting and not at all reassuring.

She stood at the window watching them cross the yard in the gathering mist. Sylvie was still clinging to his arm and at the garden gate they paused long enough for Sarah to make out their two figures standing close together in conversation, then Adam put a reassuring

137

hand on Sylvie's shoulder as if confirming some promise and they vanished into the mist.

The strange illusion of total disappearance revived Sarah's more pressing anxieties. Just so had Willie been swallowed up without sight or sound and was still out there on the moor, caught in a bog, perhaps, or trapped in the old tin-workings where she had found the dead ewe and her lamb. The farmer and his threats seemed less alarming now than the nameless perils which could overtake the wild creatures of the moor, and Willie with his one eye was already handicapped. Her fears re-doubled, Sarah bundled her journal into a hasty semblance of order on the table, opened the window to provide exit for the crow in her absence, and snatching an ancient anorak from its hook on the door ran down-stairs.

It seemed to take a long time to get as far as Ram's Tor, where she paused to catch her breath before starting to shout. As she moved on to follow the track which would lead her down to Lovacombe farm, she heard a man's voice shouting to her from the way she had come and turned thankfully back. Jed must have returned from whatever errand had taken him away and on being told of Willie's absence would have known at once where she had gone.

"I'm here!" she shouted back joyfully. "Just above Ram's Tor — I'll wait for you." She waited impatiently, listening for sounds of his progress, rewarded every so often by the scrape of a dislodged stone and the snap and rustle of trampled bracken, and when at last a man's figure took shape through the milky curtain of mist she stumbled forwards gladly, crying:

"Jed! I knew you wouldn't have failed me if only I could have found you ..."

But it was not Jed's hands which caught and steadied her, nor was it Jed's voice which replied on a note of dry exasperation:

138

"Sorry to disappoint you. What on earth possessed you to set off on a wild goose-chase in weather like this?"

"Oh, it's you . . ." she said a little blankly. She had expected to be scolded, but she had been sure of comfort too; there would be no comfort from a man who had evidently felt impelled to come after her out of consideration for his host.

"Willie's been missing for hours. Hattie said he would come back when it was time for his supper, but I couldn't wait," she said then in a rather small voice, and Adam gave her a shake.

"And Hattie was doubtless right. Now be sensible, Sarah, and come home. If we hadn't seen you go over the wall, you mightn't have been missed until it was too late. I can't imagine what good you thought you'd do beyond getting yourself lost and creating trouble for everyone," he said, and she tried to pull away.

"I'm not likely to get lost between Slattery and Lovacombe, even in fog. You forget I'm moor-bred," she replied coldly, and his hands tightened on hers.

"You're not only moor-bred but as stubborn as they come. Even sheep and ponies have been known to end up in a bog in weather like this and I, for one, wouldn't care to be obliged to organise a search-party in the middle of the night," he said with some astringency.

There seemed no point in further argument, and indeed, Sarah was grateful for his company, but as they made their cautious way along the rough, winding track she had time to remember all the awkward implications of Sylvie's earlier remarks. It had been only too clear that he had, as Sylvie intended, taken the suggestion that reading bits of her journal aloud was a joke at his expense, and if it was not so clear how he reacted to the matter of his letters, there was no doubt about the fate of her own. She supposed that she would have been as relieved as Sylvie that there was no danger now of being

139

confronted with the written word, but she was conscious of disappointment all the same.

"Adam —" she said suddenly, and stopped. It was not possible, of course, to allude to anything that had been said in the stable-room without creating further misconceptions. Sylvie would have undoubtedly followed up her advantage when they got back to the house and she had no wish to lay herself open to charges of mischief-making.

He did not, however, enquire what she had been going to say, but advised her somewhat obscurely to let sleeping dogs lie.

"There's no sense in forcing issues on any matter until the time is ripe," he said. "And talking of sleeping dogs, hadn't you better stop and do some more whistling?"

"You do the whistling, and I'll shout. My whistle seems to have dried up on me," she said, relieved that he evidently had no wish to reopen the subject, and began to call. Adam's whistle was clear and penetrating and surprisingly sweet and drew an answering pipe from some bird hidden in the undergrowth. But shout and whistle as they might there was no other sound in reply, and Sarah began to hurry ahead with incautious haste so that every so often she stumbled and finally fell down in a patch of marshy ground which had sucked her feet from under her.

"There! You see what can come of injudicious boasting!" Adam said severely as he pulled her out. "It's just as well I'm here, for all your dislike of my company."

"Oh, Adam, that isn't true!" she exclaimed with such naked distress that he put a comforting arm about her. "If I've made you feel that, it's only because — because —"

"I know why, so don't let it trouble you," he said gently, but having gone so far she had to rid herself of the burden she had carried since the night of Goose Fair.

140

"You *don't* know," she said a little distractedly. "You thought I'd fallen for Nick and let you kiss me as a kind of compensation."

"I seem to remember you accused me of a like practice," he retorted with a touch of humour, and she sighed.

"Yes, well ... that was a little different. Your affections were already engaged and Sylvie may have treated you badly."

"That's not what you thought at the time, might I remind you without being ungallant. As I remember it you declared you were tired of being a stooge and were hanged if you were going to oblige either of us to make up for presumed disappointments."

"Well, you made me good and mad with all your hamfisted advice!"

"So good and mad that you could spit — *I* know! Well, Sarah, I may have been hamfisted, but that's no excuse for avoiding me as you have, you'll admit, ever since that unfortunate night."

"I had my reasons," she said with a return to caution. "I think Goosey's best forgotten. We were a little mazed, perhaps."

"Perhaps. Some of your West Country expressions are very apt, incidentally. All the same, Sarah, I've no wish to forget Goosey for several very pertinent reasons, and I hope in time you'll come to feel the same," he said, and she looked up swiftly, trying to read the expression on his face through the wreaths of mist which drifted between them. Even as half-formed queries rose to her lips, however, the sound of a shot split the muffling silence all about them, followed by a sharp yelp of a dog.

"Willie! Willie!" Sarah screamed, and plunged wildly down the track which led to Lovacombe. The lights in the farmhouse were visible now, providing a guide, or Adam, to whom the territory was strange,

141

would have been unable to catch up with her. As it was he ricked his weak ankle, which momentarily slowed him up, but he managed to seize the bobbing hood of her anorak and jerk her to a halt.

"Hold hard, you lunatic," he said harshly. "If there's someone about crazy enough to loose off a rifle in this sort of weather, you'd better not run the risk of being mistaken for an animal."

"But he's got Willie! Didn't you hear him yelp? If he isn't dead already that man will shoot again," she cried, and almost as she spoke there came the report of another shot quite close at hand. This time there was no animal cry of pain, only the eerie pattering of cloven hooves as an unseen flock scattered behind the mist. Somewhere a man cursed roundly and Adam, a restraining hand firmly gripping Sarah's shoulder, shouted:

"Is that Mr. Rowe?"

"Aye, who wants me?" came back the surly answer, and presently a man's figure loomed out of the mist, a rifle tucked under his arm. "If you'm one of they meddlin' police inspectors from the town, I have me licence and this is my land."

"I'm nothing to do with the police, but you must be mad, taking pot shots in weather like this. You could just as easily have hit one of us."

"Oh, there be two of you — let's have a closer look. I don't take to strangers on my land any more than to sheep-worrying curs ... ah, 'tes the sharp-spoken li'l maid over to Slattery, I see. I told 'e I'd do for that tyke of yourn if I caught him at it again."

"Have you killed him?" Sarah asked quite quietly, and the farmer spat into the bracken.

"No such luck. Missed 'un in this dratted fog, more's the pity."

"But I heard him yelp."

"And so would you, young miss, if you'd had your
142

backside peppered with shot," Rowe chuckled, and Adam Adam took a deliberate step forward.

"I would advise you to keep a civil tongue in your head if you're trying to jusify your action. I'm well aware that sheep-running is a serious matter and you're within your rights to protect your property, but proof is required just the same. I understand that you've been threatening this young lady with drastic measures if you so much as caught a glimpse of her dog, and that amounts to criminal intent."

He had spoken with the unmistakable voice of authority and Rowe responded instinctively. Like all bullies, his bravado dwindled in the face of calm opposition and he began to bluster.

"I was only throwing a scar into 'un to pay back for the trouble her made for me in the first place. I wouldn't have done it if it come to the test."

"But you *have* done it!" shouted Sarah, unable to contain her frantic fears any longer. "Oh, Adam, don't just stand there bandying words with this — this *monster*! Willie may be lying wounded somewhere and we've got to find him."

"Oh, give over!" exclaimed the farmer, sounding suddenly sheepish. " 'Tweren't your Willie, dang his one eye! 'Twere that same black lurcher from the gypsy encampment, and like as not 'e's home already."

"Oh . . ." There was such relief and such humble gratitude in the soft exclamation that as she shook herself free from Adam's grasp he quite expected her to throw her arms round the man's neck in a rush of forgiveness, but she paused with her feet apart and her hands thrust into the pockets of her jeans and looked him squarely in the face.

"I will apologize for calling you a monster without due cause, Mr. Rowe, but I won't take back what I said at the time you were so unpleasant to me. Now, perhaps, you'll admit that my dog was blamed for the lurcher's sins which, of course, we guessed all along," she said, and he slapped his thigh and laughed.

"Beggared if I don't like your spirit, m'dear," he said and turned to Adam. "I know who you be now, sir — pity you've come courtin' t'other young maid — her's not so particular for all I hears tell, and there's more to taking a wife to your bed than the pleasure in a fine pair of eyes."

"Very true, Mr. Rowe, and I commend your sagacity," said Adam humorously, but Sarah, who was paying little attention, broke in impatiently:

"But where *is* Willie? We've hunted and called and whistled and never a sound. As you didn't shoot him after all, Mr. Rowe, did you ever *see* him?"

"Yes, I seed him," the farmer replied slowly, sounding a little embarrassed. "Had the varmint shut up in me barn for the past hour or more. Caught 'e and that lurcher larking about round the sheep and having me suspicion which one of 'un was a killer coaxed your beauty into the barn with a nice bit o' meat, then laid in wait for t'other. I'd of let 'un go in the morning if the weather cleared."

"*Oh!*" cried Sarah again, and this time she did make a quick dash and gave the man a hasty peck on the cheek. "Dear Mr. Rowe, I'll never again call you a monster, and now please will you release him and we can go home? Poor Mr. Soames has been most kind in insisting on helping me search, but I'm sure he's only too anxious to get back to more rewarding ways of spending the evening."

"Why, beggar me!" the farmer exclaimed, rubbing his cheek awkwardly, "danged if I don't send 'un home with one o' me nice plump fowls for that! Come you up to the house, missy, while I get 'un trussed for 'e."

It took all Adam's diplomacy to refuse the gift without giving offence, but he could see that Sarah was

144

fretting to get away, and presently after an ecstatic and somewhat hysterical reunion with Willie, they set off for home with the dog firmly secured on a length of cord.

At first Sarah had chattered away with the garrulous inconsequence which can follow on relief, but after a while reaction set in and she fell silent, aware that Adam's responses had been brief and rather abstracted, and remembering that he would be leaving them in a few days and was doubtless grudging time wasted on a wild goose chase when he could have been better employed in pursuing his aims with Sylvie. He was limping a little, she noticed, but when she expressed concern he replied with such abrupt irritation that she felt guilty, not only of tactlessness, but of being the unwitting cause of his discomfort.

She was conscious of discomfort herself as the lighted windows of Slattery pricked through the foggy dusk, announcing the end of their journey. She had already walked to the village and back in the morning to take over extra duties with the handicapped children; her legs were aching and there was probably a blister on her heel. She felt all at once as she used to feel as a child when Sylvie had commanded all the attention after some shared mishap which had resulted only in scoldings for her. Now it was Adam, who doubtless was tacitly blaming her for the thoughtless behaviour which had brought him out after her, and, as on those other occasions, she desired to hide herself in the stable-room until adult displeasure was forgotten.

"You're tired, aren't you?" he said suddenly as they reached the house, and she found the unexpected tenderness in his voice more upsetting than his earlier impatience. "I'm going to find you a drink and tuck you up beside the fire, as soon as you've settled Willie in the kitchen."

"No," she said, hoping her voice did not sound as

145

shaky as it felt, "I'm going up to the stable-room. I shall feed him there, so you go on in and get a drink for yourself."

He did not argue, for which she was grateful, but when the front door closed upon him and she was left standing under the vine-covered portico where once he had held her against him and so unthinkingly stolen her heart, she felt herself rejected.

Up in the stable-room she lighted the lamp and the paraffin stove, then kicked off her shoes to ease her aching feet.

Having attended to Willie's needs, she was wrestling with the stove which kept going out when she heard a step on the stairs outside and that clear, authoritative whistle which had sounded so sweet out on the moor. She sat back on her heels, a lighted match unheeded in her fingers, as Adam pushed open the door without knocking, then kicked it to behind him. He had evidently changed his damp clothes in a hurry, for a silk scarf was knotted casually round his throat in lieu of a collar and tie and he had a bottle of whisky tucked firmly under his arm.

Sarah exclaimed "Ow!" as she hurriedly dropped the match which was burning her fingers, and Adam stood the bottle on the table, then went on his knees beside her.

"Well now," he said, taking the matches from her, "you don't seem to be having much success with this. Didn't they teach you the rudimentaries of camping in the Brownies?"

"I never was a Brownie." she answered quite literally, and he laughed.

"We both need a drink, my child, so get up off the floor and find some glasses," he said briskly, and she scrambled slowly to her feet.

"There aren't any," she said. "Will cups do?"

"I daresay they won't impair the medicinal value of a stiff tot of whisky," he said, drawing the curtains across

146

the window. "I should have brought glasses, I suppose, but I was in a hurry."

"Were you, Adam?" she said, selecting a couple of cups from her miscellaneous assortment of crockery and setting them down on the paper-strewn table which brought back a sharp reminder of that earlier attention over her journal.

"Naturally. You didn't suppose I was going to settle fatly by the family fireside and leave you to sulk in cold discomfort, did you?"

"I never sulk."

"No, I don't believe you do. Still and all, you were giving me an undeserved brush-off, considering I'd shared your perils on the moor."

He was pouring whisky into the cups as he spoke and she watched him unhappily.

"It wasn't a brush-off," she said carefully. "I thought you seemed annoyed on the way home and were in a hurry to get back to Sylvie."

"Did you, now? Well, for your information your cousin is pleasantly occupied in experimenting with a fresh hair-do, so I've hardly been missed."

"Oh! If you were just giving in to a kindly after-thought by way of consoling yourself, you needn't have bothered," she said, and the look he gave her carried a distinct warning.

"I trust we're not going to have a repetition of the nonsense you talked on the night of Goose Fair. Here, drink this up. It may go to your head, but it will at least warm the cockles of your heart," he said, putting a cup into her hands.

"The cockles of my heart are behaving rather strangely as it is. I wouldn't like to answer for what raw spirit might do to them," she answered between sips, and he nodded approval.

"That's better. We will reopen a discussion on that interesting subject when the time is ripe. For the present we had best stick to mundane matters. Do you know you're steaming?"

She looked down at her bedraggled jeans which, being old and rather thin, had absorbed the moisture so thoroughly that she might have been out in a shower of rain.

"I think they've shrunk," she said, regarding her legs with interest, and Adam, after inspecting the assortment of garments which hung on the door as an overflow from Sarah's wardrobe in case of need, snatched a skirt off its peg and tossed it over to her.

"Here, for heaven's sake get out of those sopping pants before you get chilled," he said, then laughed at her astonished face. "Don't mind me, I'll turn my back."

He was as good as his word, and Sarah struggled out of her jeans and into the skirt with a strong desire to giggle.

"You can turn round now, Professor," she told him when she had mastered this adolescent inclination. "Not that I would have minded you looking — I was perfectly decent underneath."

"I'm glad to hear it. Well, now that you're more or less clad and in your right mind again, suppose you sit down and relax and unburden your soul," he said, turning the armchair round to the stove.

"Unburden my s-soul?" she stammered, and he pushed her into the chair.

"Figuratively speaking, of course," he said, refilling her cup and thrusting it into her hands. "I'm under the impression that this has been something of a day for you, one way and another, and it never hurts to unburden."

The day's chain of emotional disturbances returned in a tangled sequence and she suddenly wanted to cry. It wasn't fair, she thought with the dumb resentment of her childhood, that she must refuse the comfort so temptingly offered because Sylvie would always stand

148

between them; it wasn't even possible any longer to accept the friendship he was trying so patiently to establish to cement their future relationship.

"Well?" he prompted, watching her high forehead crease in that familiar pattern of anxiety which in a measure betrayed her thoughts. "Am I so difficult to confide in?"

It would be as easy, she thought, to confide in him in the flesh as it had been when he was the unknown stranger to whom she had written so freely, but it would never do to snatch at a moment of weakness in order to ease her sore spirit.

"No, dear Professor, you're a model of tact and understanding, considering you're under no obligation to bear with the rude little cousin's tiresome behaviour," she said, hoping she sounded both composed and disinterested, and his eyebrows went up.

"Still on your high horse, I take it, despite my praiseworthy efforts to save you from double pneumonia," he said lightly. "Forget it, Sarah. The rude little cousin is entitled to her reservations, after all."

She put her half-empty cup down on the table for the raw spirit seemed to aggravate the lump in her throat which was threatening to become unmanageable.

"My high horse is only a kind of friendly familiar, like a witch's cat," she said, wanting to explain her seeming ungraciousness without betraying her feelings. "You see, when perfection is the rule rather than the exception in a household, those without it take to high horses for their own protection."

"What a pity to make such a fetish of physical beauty and call it perfection," Adam said quietly, and she looked puzzled.

"But beauty *is* perfection of a kind, surely?" she said, and he smiled a little wryly.

"Yes, of a kind — but one needs a little more to justify complete subjugation. You haven't, any of you,
149

done Sylvie a service by turning her into a female Narcissus, you know."

"What an extraordinary thing to say! Aren't you in love with her?"

"One can fall in love with the most unsuitable persons for one's own comfort," he replied with some dryness, and she sighed. It seemed that although he realized his dream had been something of an illusion, he was still sufficiently enslaved to risk being hurt.

"Yes, one can," she said with such heartfelt agreement that his eyebrows went up again.

"You speak with feeling. Perhaps I wasn't so far wrong on the night of Goosey," he said, and she began to feel cornered.

"You could have been both right and wrong," she retorted, trying to capture his own trick of replying to a remark ambiguously. "Did you know Nick is going back to his wife?"

"It's been made reasonably clear to me. Your cousin is not very subtle, you'll agree."

Sarah frowned. "No, she isn't. All the same, she was fond of Nick. I think she might have married him had he been free," she said. At least he should be made to understand that Sylvie's behaviour was not entirely a matter of thoughtless vanity.

"Loyal little cuss, aren't you?" he replied with a touch of tender amusement. "You concern yourself too much with other people's feelings."

"Do I? Oh, well, it's probably the little mother coming out in me, or something," she said, trying to ignore the growing restriction in her throat. "I'm not very successful when I step out of character."

"Perhaps you try too hard."

"I've always tried too hard," she said, forgetting to preserve her flippancy as she faced an unpalatable truth. "People don't want affection thrust upon them — it's embarrassing — that spastic child I've been trying to win over for weeks told me only this morning to go and get lost. . . ."

"Poor Sarah . . . poor starved little hedgehog with so much to give . . ." Adam said softly. "Why don't you have a good cry and have done with it? I'll turn my back again if my presence will shame you."

His gentleness was almost her undoing, but as usual the tears remained obdurate, only the lump in her throat seemed to swell to unbearable proportions so that she knew she would have to choke and splutter.

"Would you get me some water?" she asked in a small voice. "My tongue always dries up when I can't cry. I'll be all right in a minute."

"I know. Something sticks in your throat and ties itself in knots," he said, filling a clean cup from the tap over the sink.

"How did you know?" she asked between fevered gulps from the cup he handed her.

"You told me."

"Did I? When?"

"A long time ago; you wouldn't remember."

She thought he was looking at her with a very curious expression, but she was so busy conquering a weakness which she felt instinctively would result in shameful admissions of the truth, should she give way to it, that she paid little attention.

"Better?" he asked when she handed back the empty cup, and she nodded. She was aware that her eyes must be watering, but at least her voice was steady.

"I'm sorry, Adam," she said, "I haven't Sylvie's gift for beautiful tears, so I try not to cry."

"Rather too successfully for comfort. Grief when it's deeply felt is seldom beautiful, only moving," he said, and turned away to rinse out the cup before she could think of a reply. Willie, having received no encouragement to proceed with repeated bids for attention, had consoled himself by chewing up Sarah's hat. Adam bent

151

down to clear up the litter of paper and bits of felt and idly smoothed out a crumpled sheet of foolscap.

"This would appear to be a piece of your journal," he said, and Sarah looked up quickly, ready to snatch it away, then leaned back in the chair, tucking her long legs under her.

"Oh, that's very ancient stuff, it's written in longhand," she said comfortably. "I only took to typing it after Sylvie and I had taken a secretarial course in Tawstock — to keep in practice, you know."

"What an odd thing to embark on when there was no question of either of you taking a job," Adam said, spreading the paper under the lamp to scan the closely-written lines.

"Well, it was Aunt Fran's doing, really. I don't think Father was much sold on the idea, but she managed to persuade him that he might find it useful himself if one of us could do a bit of typing for him when the muse came upon him. The muse hasn't obliged, of course, so it's all rather wasted."

"A pity. A job of work might have been the answer for Sylvie."

"What on earth makes you say that?" she exclaimed, really startled. "To begin with Father wouldn't hear of it and to be honest, Sylvie wouldn't like it. She's been conditioned to soft living all her life — in India, ayahs and bearers and things — and here, Slattery, if dull, provides a pleasant cocoon if you want to be lazy and queen it a bit."

He glanced up for a moment with a wry little smile and observed ambiguously:

"Very astute of you, but pleasant cocoons don't provide much scope for working off one's potentials. One might tend to assert one's individuality with too little regard for wisdom."

Her forehead wrinkled again in those anxious criss-cross lines and she said cautiously:

152

"There's always gossip when a girl is both lovely and — and irresistible to men. Sylvie can't help herself, you know — she has to be admired and petted, but her conquests don't mean very much — and after all" — she finished naively — "it would be a very large feather in the cap of the man who finally wins her, shouldn't you think?"

He laughed and his eyes were a little mocking.

"A very large feather indeed, if that were all. Don't think me unappreciative of your lovely cousin's undoubted talent for collecting scalps — I can only regret that the field is so small," he said, and returned to his occupation with the tattered pages of foolscap.

"You make your capital S exactly like Sylvie's. Did you know?" she heard him say suddenly, and was immediately wide awake.

"I used to admire her flourishes when we were at school and try to copy them," she replied rather hurriedly, and found he was looking at her with a decidedly odd expression.

"Did you, indeed? Very successfully, I may say — no one would know the difference."

"Well, perhaps some of my capitals aren't a bad imitation, but our handwriting isn't really at all alike."

"No? Well, I can hardly dispute that, can I, since her letters were always typed — to keep in practice, I presume?"

"Yes, of course. I started typing my journal for the same reason — oh, I've told you that. You'd be surprised how efficient one becomes after only quite a little while."

"I would indeed, and still more surprised if what I suspect isn't true. You wrote those letters, didn't you, Sarah?"

The question had been asked with such deceptive quietness that for a moment she thought she must have

153

misheard him, but his face in the lamplight had the grave hardness of certainty and she just sat there staring at him and saying nothing.

"Well?"

"How long have you known?" she asked in a very small voice.

"Does it matter? What is important is why."

"I don't know that I can explain," she said, pushing agitated fingers through her damp brown hair. "Sylvie, you see, isn't very good at keeping up a correspondence, so when she seemed like letting it drop, I just took over."

"I see. And why couldn't that have been explained at the time?"

"Well, it wouldn't have been the same, would it? You had fallen for Sylvie and it seemed only kind to go on pretending." Even to Sarah it sounded childish and she was not surprised at his reaction.

"It seemed only *kind*! What did you take me for? A lovesick youth to be bolstered up with a lot of phoney nonsense?" he said, suddenly exploding into anger.

"The letters weren't phoney, even if they did read like nonsense," she said, trying to whip up a like indignation, but his face was again the face of a stranger, as it had seemed caught in the spotlight on the night of Goose Fair, and she could find no stomach for retaliation. For the first time she could appreciate the folly of that well-intentioned deception, and not only the folly, but the arrogance in fobbing off a grown man with the soothing syrup one might mete out to a child.

"I'm sorry ..." she said with weary acceptance, "I suppose neither of us thought the affair was going to lead to anything, but I'm sorry, all the same. I only took over the letters because it seemed mean not to stick to a bargain which didn't call for very much effort.... I imagined you lonely, you see."

"And you were lonely yourself, of course," Adam said, and his mood suddenly altered. He stood looking down at her curled dejectedly in the dilapidated chair and the beginnings of a smile touched the corners of his mouth. She was looking her plainest with the freckles standing out on skin which showed sallow in the lamp-light, for her summer tan had reached an unbecoming stage; but her hair, fast drying in the warmth of the room, was beginning to curl all over her head with a disarming charm.

"I suppose I was," she said, answering his question which had been more in the manner of a statement. "At first, you see, you were just a sort of substitute for my journal, then later —"

"Yes?"

"Oh, well, it doesn't matter now. It's just as well you destroyed the letters."

"You won't get off as lightly as that, young woman," he said with an encouraging return to his more familiar manner, and thrusting a hand into the breast pocket of his jacket, extracted a packet of rubber-banded letters and threw it down on the table.

"But you told Sylvie you hadn't kept her letters," Sarah said, eyeing the evidence of her guilt with much misgiving.

"I only spoke the truth — she didn't write them," he replied calmly, then shook his head at her. "You weren't very clever over your deception, were you? It didn't seem to occur to you that an abrupt change of style and mood might occasion surprise."

"Well, it evidently didn't occur to you either," she retorted, recovering something of her old spirit, and the humour left his eyes.

"Oh, yes, it occurred to me. Unfortunately, I mistook the change of manner for a change of heart, which was hardly surprising since I'd no reason to think otherwise. Do you realize, I wonder, how much of yourself you betrayed when you wrote those letters?"

"If I did, then it's probably false reasoning on your part, Professor. Don't forget it was Sylvie you had in mind when you read them," she said with more tartness than she intended, but at all costs she must stick to her role of the plain little cousin with mistaken ideas on chivalry and keep him from guessing at her own change of heart.

"Very true, but natural mistakes can be remedied without undue loss if one brings a little intelligence to bear on the subject. I had begun to hope, you see —"

"Hope what?" she asked as he paused, but he had been quicker than she to catch the sound of a footstep on the outside staircase and it was only a matter of seconds before Willie gave his usual warning and plunged, barking, towards the door.

Sarah began to scramble out of the chair, teased by an impression that all this had happened before. In a moment Sylvie would demand querulously whether Adam was up there, Willie would snap at her ankles and tear her stocking, and she would make a small scene for Adam, then flounce off in a huff.

None of it happened quite like that, however. Adam seized and subdued Willie before the door opened, and Sylvie, when she stepped inside, seemed more anxious than cross. If she read more into the little scene she had interrupted than she cared for, she was careful this time to refrain from comment and said quickly:

"Are you all right, Sarah? Hattie said Adam was worried about you and was bringing you a drink to warm you up, but that was hours ago, and Aunt Fran thought you might be ill. It really *was* rather crazy to go chasing over the moor in weather like this."

"Yes, I suppose it was," Sarah agreed meekly, touched and rather surprised that her family should feel concern for her when they were quite accustomed to her independent comings and goings.

156

"Well, I think you'd both better come back to the house, now. Hattie's got the water good and hot for baths, and Uncle Gil has taken his cold to bed, so we're all going to picnic informally by the living-room fire, which will be rather fun. Aunt Fran's getting quite girlish at the prospect of a nice cosy get-together and you won't mind letting your back hair down, for once, with a parcel of giggling females, will you, Adam?"

"I can't see your aunt giggling like an overgrown schoolgirl, but it sounds an attractive programme," Adam replied with a smile, and looked relieved. If he had been interrupted at a moment when he might have said more than was wise, he was probably grateful for Sylvie's intervention, Sarah thought, wondering when he would make the opportunity for a showdown with her. She had not long to wonder, however, for Sylvie's sharp eyes almost at once saw the packet of letters lying on the table and she snatched them up, exclaiming merrily:

"Oh, my letters! You *did* keep them, after all, you wicked tease! Now, Sarah love, you can do no less than disgorge Adam's."

Sarah did not reply, waiting to see that Adam would say, but he made no comment either and stood warming his back at the stove, continuing to observe Sylvie with a distinctly appreciative eye.

"May I borrow them, dear Professor? I'd like to refresh my memory and find out how many incriminating things I may have said," Sylvie went on, her eyes sparkling with anticipation as she began stuffing the letters into a pocket of the coat she had flung round her shoulders.

"Save the act for another time. He knows about the letters," Sarah said, unwilling to allow her cousin to humiliate herself further. At first Sylvie's lovely face registered nothing but blankness, then two angry spots of colour showed in her cheeks.

"So you told him," she said in a soft little voice. "I

didn't think you would be so mean just to get a bit of your own back."

"Sarah didn't tell me, there was no need," Adam said, speaking at last, and Sylvie whirled round on him.

"What do you mean, there was no need?" she demanded, and there was the suspicion of a tremor in her voice. "How could you have known if she didn't tell you?"

"Not really very difficult, if you think back," he said quite gently. "You both of you reacted rather oddly to any mention of the letters — besides, you didn't quite measure up to them, if you'll forgive me, Sylvie."

Sarah gave him a quick, startled glance, wondering if she had read more into that remark than he had intended, but Sylvie evidently missed any personal implication, for she said a little breathlessly:

"I don't know what you think you mean by that. I may have teased you and flirted a bit to keep you guessing, but you weren't very quick off the mark, were you? Perhaps you aren't in love after all — or are you?"

"Perhaps you and I mean different things by that," he said. "You should grow up, my dear."

"Grow up!" she was getting angry and forgot her coquettish pose in a burst of offended dignity. "I'm not a child who can't recognize the signs when a man's attracted to me, and you, I might say, gave a pretty fair imitation of a would-be suitor when you first came here. Anyway, I can't see how those stupid letters should make any difference."

"No, I don't suppose you do. Just for interest, why did you keep up the fiction? It's given your uncle and aunt a very false idea of the situation, to say nothing of myself."

Sylvie's eyes had already filled with tears and her mouth began to pucker.

"Oh, *Adam*! It's all been a silly mistake!" she cried. "The whole thing started as a joke, but I see now I should never have let Sarah persuade me."

"A joke? Dear me, what an odd sense of humour you must have."

"It was Sarah's idea, not mine. She said let's swop places just for a giggle and see if your silly old professor notices any difference, and then when you didn't seem to, she wouldn't give it up because she got some kind of kick out of it, and there didn't seem much point in me writing as well and — and I suppose I thought it was one of those sort of silly pen-friend affairs that would just die out. I'd no *idea*, of course, that you'd both kept up the correspondence until you suddenly wrote to Uncle Gil and he asked you down to stay, and then it was too late to c-confess — besides, I'd rather fallen for you...."

"I see," Adam said expressionlessly when her words trailed off into silence, but Sarah, recovering her breath after the first shock of outrage, exclaimed violently:

"Sylvie, how *can* you! You know very well the suggestion came from you — because you'd just met Nick and couldn't be bothered and I took over simply because I was sorry for anyone stuck out in the wilds waiting for letters that never came. Why, you weren't even interested enough to read Adam's replies, let alone offer to write yourself."

"Oh, darling, isn't that just wishful thinking?" Sylvie said. "You've developed a teeny and quite understandable crush for our dear professor now he's here, but at the time you thought it was a huge joke to have him on — you know you did. Don't you remember how we used to spend hours up here giggling over his letters and thinking out corny replies? It wasn't very nice, I know, Adam, but I didn't really think you were serious and would come back and track me down, and it gave poor Sarah a bit of harmless fun and was an amusing change from that dreary old diary."

"No, it wasn't very nice," Adam said quietly, but

although he answered Sylvie he was looking at Sarah, and there was such naked bitterness in his eyes that she felt he had struck her.

"Well, Sarah," he said, with something of a bite in his voice, as she remained silent, "at least a modicum of entertainment has come out of this not very edifying affair. I hope you had your money's worth making a fool out of a stranger for no better reason than an adolescent desire for kicks. If you'll both excuse me, I'll go and have that bath which Hattie's laid on." He did not look at her again, but tucked the whisky bottle under his arm and went.

They both fell silent, listening to his footsteps ringing on the cobbles and dying away as he reached the garden gate, then Sarah held out a demanding hand.

"You can give me back those letters," she said in a tight repressed little voice, "since there won't be any need to refresh your memory after this. You're really rather stupid, Sylvie, as I've often thought. You shouldn't have included yourself in the joke when you were so anxious to paint me black. Adam won't like that."

"Not so stupid," Sylvie retorted, throwing the packet of letters on to the table. "I'm not so dumb that I hadn't already suspected our dear professor's interest was wandering, but I don't mind slipping a little to cook your goose for you. Now we're quits."

"How are we quits? What have I ever done to you?"

"Only tried to take what's mine. Listen, Sarah, I've lost Nick to another woman, which was humiliating enough, even if she *is* his wife, but if I've lost Adam too it's certainly not going to be to my dim little cousin. It doesn't look, now, as if I'm going to have the pleasure of turning down a proposal before he goes, which somewhat spoils the record, but at least I'll have the satisfaction of knowing that you won't get him."

"I don't know you at all," Sarah said slowly. "I can't

160

begin to understand why these petty little personal triumphs should be important to you when you have so much already."

"Well, love, that's probably your answer. One gets conditioned to being the queen bee, so these things matter," Sylvie said quite simply. The spite had gone out of her entirely and, having convinced herself that however things might turn out she had saved her pride with no great loss to herself, she was ready to smile on everyone again so long as they acknowledged defeat.

Sarah, knowing that she herself must look as plain and bedraggled as she felt, observed the unblemished perfection of her cousin's exquisite features with wonder and an odd little twist of pity. It was as if, she thought, she saw her for the first time and no longer envied an endowment which, alas, could only be transient. . . . When Sylvie grew old and men no longer desired her, the mainspring of her being would die . . .

"What are you gaping at?" Sylvie asked, her hands going at once to her hair.

"Just admiring. Nothing really shakes you, does it?" Sarah replied, and Sylvie smiled complacently, accepting the remark as a compliment.

"It doesn't do to let yourself care too much — it gives you wrinkles," she said, tucking a confiding arm through Sarah's as if that bitter little scene had never taken place. "Did you know that one of Uncle Gil's literary cronies has a son interested in old porcelain who wants to see the collection? He's coming to stay when Adam goes and Uncle is quite chuffed at being consulted as an expert . . . it will be rather fun, won't it, if this young man turns out to be a dish?"

"Yes, won't it?" Sarah agreed politely, wishing she did not feel so drained of intelligence and envying her cousin's astonishing powers of recuperation. It was easy to see that the prospect of a fresh admirer was already compensating for present disappointments and she suddenly appreciated the point of one of Adam's earlier remarks. Sylvie was, indeed, a feminine counterpart of Narcissus; it was herself she saw mirrored in the eyes of her devotees and it was her own image which dictated how much or how little she should care in return.

"Well, we'd better be getting back to the house," Sylvie said, glancing at the old kitchen clock on the mantelpiece. "I suppose it's a bit much to expect that I'll get back into Adam's good graces tonight, but I'll have a darn good try. Coming?"

"No, you go on. I must see to the stove and the lamp. Sylvie —"

"Yes, love?"

"Never mind." It was not possible to appeal to the nicety of a person who could revert to casual endearments with such an extraordinary lack of sensibility, Sarah thought, and was relieved that Sylvie was not sufficiently interested to enquire further and was already half way down the stairs. She pottered about aimlessly for a while, seeing to the routine chores, and finally placing her letters in the hiding place which she had made for Adam's. There seemed no point in returning them since he could have no further interest in them now, and later she would destroy them together with those brief replies which she had cherished for so long.

Willie seemed reluctant to leave his snug corner where he was sleeping off the day's adventures and an extra large supper, and she left him there, suspecting that there would be enough discordance in the house to fray Hattie's temper without an additional irritant in her kitchen. The fog was lifting, she saw as she clattered down the wooden steps and into the yard. She stood for a moment drawing comfort from the lighted windows of the house which had warmed and welcomed her whatever the state of her spirits, and wondered whether she would ever know that same contentment again. But the pattern did not alter although things might change, she thought. With Adam gone life at Slattery would continue much as before; Sylvie would find fresh admirers, her father, if piqued at being proved wrong, would doubtless congratulate himself on possessing the gem of his collection for a little longer, and she herself would return to the claims of her sick animals and the solace of her journal, and in time would forget the stirrings of her heart. . . .

CHAPTER IX

SARAH did not look forward to the evening and lingered over her bath as long as she dared to postpone the inevitable meeting with Adam. She wondered whether she could plead a chill and excuse herself from dinner, but Aunt Fran had keen eyes and even keener preceptions. However, it was Sylvie who took to her bed, creating a well-timed little flutter of concern, but her absence made things no easier. It was impossible with only the three of them, picnicking informally round the fire, not to make a show of sociability, although Sarah had the feeling that only the good manners of a guest prevented Adam from ignoring her altogether. She avoided his eyes whenever possible, not liking the unsmiling regard of a critical stranger which rested on her every so often.

It was a relief to have the excuse of saving Hattie's legs by clearing away when the meal was finished, but when she came back with the tray to collect the few remaining glasses, Adam was alone, lighting his pipe.

"Where's Aunt Fran?" she asked, piling glasses on to the tray which such haste that one shot into the hearth and smashed.

"Gone up to take Sylvie's temperature. It seems she's feverish," Adam replied, stooping to shovel up the broken glass.

"*Is* she!" said Sarah grimly, and picked up the tray with such violence that the glasses rattled against each other.

"Better put it down," Adam said, leaning back again and drawing on his pipe. "It's always a sign of an unquiet mind when you break things."

"And would you expect my mind to be tranquil after everything that's been said?" she retorted, both surprised and pleased to find that she could still work up a satisfactory semblance of rage despite the soreness of her heart.

"Well now, I should have thought I was the one to have a grievance, not you," he observed with disconcerting mildness. "After all, you've had your fun at my expense, so you shouldn't grudge me a little at yours. Look out! You'll drop the lot if you aren't careful, and that won't please your father."

He had, she thought, mentioned her father deliberately to remind her that she was merely an awkward child whose outrageous prank was no more important than her displays of gaucheness. She must have mistaken that bitterness in his eyes when he left them in the stable-room for a sense of disappointment in her, when clearly it was Sylvie's naive admissions which had hurt him.

"Adam —" she began awkwardly, still holding the tray and longing to get out of the room but feeling she must make some effort to straighten out his misconceptions, "Sylvie doesn't mean half she says when she wants to make a scene, you know. It wasn't like that at all — about the letters, I mean."

"Wasn't it? Well, Sarah, it scarcely matters now. I was the fool imagining nothing had been lost. Just as a matter of interest, how were you proposing to explain away the switch-over or were you proposing to keep up the farce indefinitely?"

"That was Sylvie's worry. It was up to her to put herself right in your eyes if you meant business," she said with more coolness than she felt, and he gave her a long thoughtful look.

"Which she did to some tune," he replied quite gently. "Tell me, Sarah, has the suggestion that you had formed something of a — an attachment for me as a result of

165

that correspondence any foundation, or am I being unduly conceited to ask such a question?"

He had spoken with a tentativeness which, had she not been so intent on preserving her dignity, might have signified that he was not entirely disinterested, but the events of that long and emotional day had crowded too swiftly one upon the other for clear thinking. Sarah's only desire now was to cling to her self-respect and admit nothing which could lead to embarrassment or, worse still, a kindly forbearance on his part.

"Yes, you are," she answered. "You can't help having your share of the male's natural arrogance, I suppose, but you shouldn't let Sylvie's nonsense about schoolgirl crushes go to your head. She was only getting one back at me."

"Was she, indeed? The pair of you appear to have a somewhat warped sense of humour, but doubtless my natural male arrogance is to blame for being unable to appreciate the jest."

He had spoken with a certain dry parody of her own manner, but she thought she detected a fresh note of bitterness and said defensively:

"You can't have it all ways, can you, Professor?"

"It depends on what you mean by all ways," he replied with a lift of one eyebrow. "You can hardly lay the fault at my door since I was unaware that I was being taken for a ride."

"It — it wasn't like that at all," she faltered, wanting to explain but unaware that in putting the blame where it belonged she would not only destroy such illusions as he still might have but would give herself away as well.

"No? Well, tell me this, Sarah. Was I entirely mistaken in what I read into your letters, or had you begun to think of me as a person and not just as a substitute for your journal?"

She was so tired and so driven by the necessity to

hang on to her pride at all costs that she could not recognize the opening he was offering her.

"You might remember that you read Sylvie's opinions into my letters, so naturally you were mistaken," she said. "As to finding you more worthwhile than my journal, I suppose that might be true since diaries can't afford one the satisfaction of a reply, but that's all there was to it, and the joke went sour on me."

"It's a habit jokes have when they misfire," he said in quite a different tone of voice. "Let it be a warning to you if you're ever again tempted to borrow a little glamour from your cousin."

"I will, and thank you for reminding me of my proper place," said Sarah, and marched out of the room with the rattling tray of glasses, satisfied that although she had outraged every tender sensibility she possessed, he was finally rid of any suspicions he might have had as to the true state of her heart.

Frances, who had lingered upstairs in order to give the two of them time to straighten out whatever was causing this state of tension, heard the glasses being carried out to the kitchen and came down again. She found the guest scowling into the fire and acknowledging her return rather absently, but she said nothing and sat down opposite him with a fresh pile of mending.

"Miss Fran, I think I should take my leave of you a few days earlier than was planned," Adam said abruptly, and she glanced across at him with no noticeable indication of surprise.

"Yes," she said, screwing up her eye while she threaded a needle. "Well, we will be sorry to lose you, naturally, but I daresay you would like to be on the spot before you actually have to start work. When do you think of leaving us?"

"Tomorrow, if the weather's cleared and I won't upset any arrangements."

"We have no arrangements as far as I know. Will you

see Sylvie before you go? I shall probably keep her in bed tomorrow as a precaution."

"Is she ill?"

"Not ill — just a little feverish and upset. She can run a slight temperature as easily as she can turn on tears, you know. Neither tendency is a trick, she's just highly strung. Have you told Sarah you're going tomorrow?"

"No."

"I hope," said Fran, carefully after a pause, "you aren't allowing yourself to be influenced by any foolishness on Sylvie's part. It would be a pity to throw away something fundamental for want of a little understanding."

"I'm sorry, Miss Fran, if in accepting your hospitality I've misled you," he replied gently. "My decision to leave isn't the result of a lovers' tiff, however."

"You misunderstand me," she said with equal gentleness. "I didn't suppose you had given in to my brother's persuasions for the sake of furthering your suit with Sylvie."

"Didn't you?"

"No. Even so I may have been wrong . . . certainly I may have been wrong on one count. I haven't the same certainty about a man's sensibilities as I have for another woman's . . . Sarah *is* a woman, you know, for all she may seem young and naive and sometimes rather gauche. Now I've broken the habit of years and entered into personalities, which could be impertinent. Forgive me, and put it down to the foolish misconceptions of a spinster aunt long past the age of romantic dreaming."

"What are you trying to tell me?" he asked quietly. "I could find nothing impertinent in anything you might choose to submit."

"If not impertinent, then possibly unwise," she replied. "It's never safe to draw conclusions from unsupported evidence."

168

"And what conclusions have you drawn, Miss Fran?"

She looked up then and smiled across at him.

"That you came here seeking an image and found it, but the reality didn't measure up, for one."

"And the other?"

"The other," she said, bending once more over her work, "is more difficult to define. I had thought lately — but then it's more easy to mistake a natural fondness for something deeper, isn't it?"

"Yes. Sarah would tell you it's the male's natural arrogance to imagine love where none exists, but I'm not quite so conceited as that, even though I may have had my moments of delusion," he said with gentle humour, and her eyes as she suddenly whipped off her glasses were as wide and surprised as a young girl's.

"But don't you know she's in love with you?" she exclaimed. "When I spoke of mistaking a fondness for something else, I was thinking of you."

"A schoolgirl crush, nothing more, as Sylvie would doubtless confirm," Adam said with sudden harshness. "The joke, you see, got out of hand, and it seems the poor child lost her heart a little as an unexpected result, but she'll get over it."

"What on earth are you talking about?" Frances asked with mild astonishment. "If Sylvie's been making mischief and dismissing Sarah's feelings as a joke then it was simply sour grapes and you should know better than to believe her."

"Unfortunately the whole business was a joke at my expense. Sarah wrote those letters," he said, and she sighed, not with regret for the deception, he thought, but with relief that some hitherto puzzling matter was at last explained.

"I always knew there was something fishy about those letters," she said with a satisfied air. "It was quite out of character for Sylvie to persevere with anything so tedious as letter-writing once the novelty had worn off, and she

169

seemed much too taken up with the fascinating Mr. Bannister to trouble about a stranger she had only met once. I imagine in Sarah's eyes you would have seemed like a lame duck who needed caring for and she just took over. Can you only feel you've been made a fool of, Adam?"

"Not until today. You see, I think I fell in love with the writer of the letters, not the visual image I had carried around with me. It took a little working out to arrive at the truth, but as I came to know Sarah it was not difficult to guess that for some reason there had been a switch over. Sylvie could never have written those letters."

"Then what has happened today to cause you such disillusion that you must rush off tomorrow without a word of explanation?"

"Sarah needs no explanation. The whole thing started as an adolescent prank and went on that way. The two of them used to read the letters aloud to each other and enjoy a good laugh."

"That I won't believe, and if Sylvie invented such rubbish for your edification it was simply her way of absolving herself and putting a spoke in Sarah's wheel at the same time."

"That would be nice to believe, but Sarah admitted it only just now, together with the information that the joke had gone sour on her, so you can hardly blame me for not wanting to make a fool of myself a second time," he said, sounding suddenly very tired, and Frances hesitated.

"Oh, my dear good man!" she exclaimed then with her first touch of impatience, "can't you understand that a young girl's pride is just as stubborn as your own, and far more vulnerable at that age? If you hadn't given her any indication of your changed feelings she'd naturally do all she could not to give away her own."

"You think I'm being unreasonable and rather

childish, don't you, Miss Fran?" he said, and she picked up the neglected garment in her lap and started stitching again.

"All men are children, which is one of those tiresome clichés women like to make use of but have a grain of truth in them all the same," she answered briskly. "You wouldn't be so upset by this idiotic business if you didn't care, you know. I'm beginning to hope my poor, plain Sarah's affections aren't so misplaced after all. She's badly in need of a respectable father-figure, if nothing else to make up for past omissions."

"I have no inclination to act as a respectable father-figure to any young woman I may marry, neither do I think, from past experience, that your poor, plain Sarah would be content with that," Adam observed with a touch of possessive restraint that made her smile.

"No, she wouldn't," she agreed calmly, "but you're going to have your work cut out convincing her of that before you leave tomorrow, so perhaps you'd better postpone your departure for another day."

"Perhaps I had," he said with a quick grin, and got up, "but there's no harm in beginning now, is there? It's even money that she'll be visiting Willie in the stable-room before going to bed, so if you'll excuse me I'll go and lie in wait."

But he waited in vain. Sarah for once had gone upstairs without concern for Willie.

The door of Sylvie's room was open and she paused for a moment as her cousin called to her. Sylvie was propped up against her pillows looking pale and ethereal in the soft light of the lamp. She wore her most becoming bed-jacket and her face was freshly made up.

"Would you go down again, love, and ask Adam to come up and say goodnight?" she said. "I — I'd like to explain about the letters before I go to sleep."

"Explain what?"

"Why, that I'd been a teeny bit unfair to you, of

171

course — to confess that I'd just been too lazy to bother and — and ask forgiveness. Why are you looking at me like that?"

"Because I'm through with being the plain little cousin who can be whistled back when it suits," Sarah said quite pleasantly. "I don't for a moment believe you'd tell Adam the truth out of cousinly concern for me, but if you're all set for a romantic bedroom scene, still hoping for a last-minute declaration, you'd better ring the bell and get Hattie to take your message down. Good night."

"*Sarah!*" The reproach in Sylvie's voice was quite genuine and tears had already sprung to her eyes, but Sarah just smiled at her with the tolerant indifference an adult might bestow upon a tiresome, exacting child and went away.

Although sleep had come upon her so swiftly, oblit-crating all conscious thought, her unquiet spirit must have troubled her dreams, for she awoke in the small hours with a confused sense of nightmare. If she had been dreaming, she remembered nothing but an intang-ible impression of disquieting incidents which, dream-like, had no sequence but were nonetheless disturbing, and she found herself suddenly wide awake and search-ing frantically for matches. She had knocked several objects off the bedside table before she found and lighted the candle, but the wavering flame bringing the room and its familiar landmarks into focus began to dispel the first unreasoning alarm. Her clock said only half-past two, she saw with surprise, but the wind had risen and perhaps it was that which had wakened her. She sat for a few moments with her knees drawn up to her chin, listening to the rising and falling of the gusts blowing against her window, and thinking with relief that the fog must now be dispersed, when another sound joined in; the eerie, desolate sound of a dog howling, and she sprang out of bed. Willie! How could she have forgotten Willie locked in the stable-room and waking in the small hours to unaccustomed night quarters and a sense of abandonment?

She stopped only long enough to thrust her feet into a pair of slippers and fling on an old duffle coat over her pyjamas, guiltily aware that if he should arouse the household before she could release him she would get short shrift from her father in the morning, and crept down the stairs. As she slipped out of the house she was aware that bedroom doors were already opening and voices being raised in alarm. With the dog's hysterical barking and the noise she herself had made, they must imagine Slattery was being burgled, she thought with a nervous giggle, but as she ran through the garden gate and into the yard, her natural anxiety turned to fear. Smoke was pouring from the open window of the stable-room and the dark shape of an animal leaping and twisting could be seen in grotesque silhouette against the background glare.

Sarah had no thought to run back to the house for help, as she searched frantically for the key which was always kept under a stone. As she flung herself up the staircase and fitted the key in the lock, she remembered that she had been uncertain at the time whether she had turned the wick of the stove sufficiently down, but she had been too dazed and too upset after that dreadful scene over the letters to go back and make sure. She got the door open and Willie shot past her, nearly knocking her down, and disappeared into the night, and she stumbled blindly through the smoke and debris of over-turned chairs and scattered burning papers, to the sink. It was Willie who must have started the fire, she thought, for the stove was lying on its side in a pool of burning paraffin which had already set the rug alight and was making a bonfire of the loose papers of the ill-fated journal which had been knocked on to the floor and was blazing merrily. As she kept filling a bucket

173

from the sink to douse the flames, she had time for regret at the destruction of so much that had been part of herself. It had been a day of destruction altogether, she thought wryly, and perhaps it was fitting that the journal should perish with the rest of the make-believe.

"But not my letters!" she cried aloud, trying to beat out a little tongue of flame which was licking up the side of an old shoe-box where she had hidden Adam's letters from Sylvie's prying eyes, and hit out blindly as she felt herself lifted roughly and carried to the door.

"For God's sake! What do you think you're playing at now, setting the place alight?" Adam's voice demanded furiously above her head, and she replied equally furiously:

"*I* didn't do it, it was Willie ... put me down at once, I've got to rescue something!"

"You've done enough rescuing creatures that don't need you. Stop being so damned officious," he said.

"I'm not officious and it's not creatures, so mind your own business," she snapped back, and wriggled out of his grasp and across the room. He went after her, cursing roundly, and as she snatched up the shoe-box, now well alight, she became aware of voices shouting from the yard, the sound of breaking glass as someone heaved a brick through the window, and Jed appeared suddenly in the doorway directing a jet of water from the garden hose into the room, catching her full in the chest and making her choke. It caught the box as well, swiftly reducing it to a sodden mess, and Adam deftly plucked out the contents before she had time to get back her breath and held the half-charred packet of letters high above her head.

"Is this the cause of a regrettable impulse to commit hari-kiri?" he inquired with heavy sarcasm, and before she could stop him, dropped the letters on to the still burning remains of her journal.

"Oh, *no*!" she cried, and would have gone down on

her knees to snatch them back if he had not caught her wrist in a grip which promised no mercy should she try to free herself.

"No, you don't! There's been enough trouble caused through these perishing flights of fancy — better destroy the lot together with a few unfortunate misconceptions," he said with rather grim satisfaction, and she let her wrists go limp in his grasp.

"The fire's out," she said, looking about her with surprise.

"Well, fortunately, the principal casualty appears to be your journal, which is no great loss to anyone," he said unfeelingly, and she began to tremble.

"It's a loss to me, though I don't expect you to mind about that," she retaliated, trying to keep her teeth from chattering. "Why are you going out of your way to be so unpleasant?"

"Because, my dearest, you are a little more shocked than you realize, and since I don't feel like slapping you into a state of reason at this particular moment I must content myself with a little harsh speaking," he said, very gently, and she looked up into his dark face so suddenly creased into little lines of tenderness and her eyes filled with tears.

"You see?" he said, touching her wet lashes with an admonitory finger. "It wouldn't take much to encourage those hitherto difficult tears, would it? Perhaps I may yet be able to do you a good turn by releasing them, but I think we'll defer such experiments until we find ourselves in more comfortable surroundings."

"What did you call me?" she asked, beginning to feel a little light-headed, and he frowned.

"I don't think I was guilty of alluding to you as a hedgehog again, though one never can tell what may slip out in the heat of the moment," he replied quite seriously.

"Then it probably *was* a slip — in the heat of the

moment," she said, "but like it or not, you addressed me as your dearest."

"Did I, indeed? Well, it's a step in the right direction, wouldn't you agree?"

"It depends on the direction," she said, beginning to wonder whether all this wasn't part of the same dream which had woken her up at half-past two in the morning.

"So it does," he agreed good-humouredly, "but our direction for the moment had better be the house and a return to bed. Come on."

"Haven't you been to bed at all?" she asked, suddenly noticing that he was still dressed.

"No, I didn't feel like sleep, after vainly keeping vigil down below for you to come and let Willie out."

"*Did* you? Why?"

"To make my peace, perhaps, and help you to make yours. Anyway, I got cold and gave it up — besides, I had some packing to do."

"Packing — in the middle of the night?"

"It seemed as good a time as any since I proposed leaving in the morning if the weather cleared."

"Oh! Does Father know?"

"I daresay your aunt has told him, but naturally I shouldn't go without seeing him."

"Oh!" she said again, sounding blank and unnaturally polite. "What did Aunt Fran say?"

"Your aunt said a good many things which were much more to the point, but we won't go into that now. Come along — your teeth are chattering."

She took a last look at the blackened ruins of her journal and those controversial letters, then went without speaking into the windy night. She had read what she wished into those unexpected exchanges, thanks to the hour and her own confusion of mind, she supposed wearily. He was leaving at once because she was indirectly responsible and no man would wish to prolong a situation which had made him feel a fool.

"*Willie!*" she exclaimed, suddenly remembering as Adam joined her in the yard. "He lit off on to the moor in his fright and is probably scared to come back. I must go and look for him. . . ."

"My darling, half-witted child, you'll do no such thing!" he retorted, firmly taking her arm and marching her towards the garden gate. "That ubiquitous animal has caused enough disruption for one day, and if ever I saw a dog more able to look after its own interests it's your Willie, so for goodness' sake stop wearing out your sympathies for nothing. That dog has more lives than any cat and an unfailing nose for his own comforts. He'll be back in the morning."

"Yes, Adam," she said meekly, "but I wish you wouldn't go on using endearments you don't mean."

"If you consider being called half-witted an endearment then you're easy to please," he retorted. "Anyway, it's not a becoming trait to pick on a man's unintentional slips."

"No, I suppose not," she said, and stumbled. They had nearly reached the house and he stopped abruptly and picked her up, depositing her in the vine-covered porch where she had first learned so unwillingly to love him.

"You're half asleep already," he said, giving her a little shake as he set her down, "but before we go in, will you tell me this? Had things been different, would you have shown me quite so many prickles?"

The wind stirred the vine leaves to an insistent measure of taps and whispers about them, but it was too dark to see his face and she was too tired to resist any longer.

"Had things been different, dear Professor, you wouldn't have noticed my prickles," she said gently, and slipped under his arm and into the house before he could find an answer.

177

Sarah slept late into the morning, and awoke to an imperceptible air of change in the house.

"Has Adam gone?" she asked her aunt, when they met downstairs.

"Yes. He went off about an hour ago. Such a lucky thing the weather brightened for him, wasn't it?" Frances replied. She was going from room to room replenishing flower vases from a little plastic watering-can and paused to remove a drop of spilled water from one of the china cabinets.

"Yes, wasn't it?" Sarah agreed politely, and her aunt looked amused.

"You don't sound very surprised, but I suppose he tendered his farewells after all that disturbance in the night," she said.

She was more mortified than surprised. It was true he had told her he was leaving and she had no real cause to complain because he had not thought it necessary to bid her a formal farewell, but it wouldn't have hurt him, she thought, to wait until she had had her sleep out before taking his leave of them.

"How has Father taken it?" she asked.

"Adam's sudden departure, or being roused in the middle of the night?"

"I *did* try to be quiet. I didn't know then, of course, that Willie was in danger, or I wouldn't have been so careful."

"Careful! The clatter you made going downstairs was enough to waken the dead — we all thought someone had broken in! However, it was just as well as things turned out. At least it gave Adam a chance to fly to your rescue."

"As things turned out, that wasn't at all necessary. It was a very minor conflagration, and Jed soon put it out," Sarah replied, somewhat coldly, and her aunt gave a small impatient sigh.

"Dear me, you are being awkward! Adam must have

178

played his cards badly," she observed.

"There weren't any cards left to play. I suppose you know all about those wretched letters, now?"

"Yes, but I wasn't very surprised. I'd always thought there was something bogus about that unlikely correspondence. Are you determined on being stubborn, Sarah?"

"I don't know what you mean. I'm sorry Adam got the wrong impression, but I'm not sorry he found out. Sylvie would never have done for him."

"I fancy he'd already discovered that for himself," Frances said a little dryly. "Sylvie wasn't being very clever if she hoped to gain anything by keeping up this ridiculous farce, and you were a still bigger fool to go along with her."

"Yes, I suppose I was, only — well, he seemed to have no doubts of his feelings right from the start and — and I hoped very much things would work out."

"Very praiseworthy and extremely shortsighted. Surely you know by now that all Sylvie wants is another scalp? I don't say she wouldn't have accepted Adam, since young Mr. Bannister seems, rather fortunately, to have let her down, but I suspect that Adam knew it, too. You have to be very much in love, my dear, to be content with someone else's crumbs."

"And Adam can't be, after all — in love, I mean — so that makes me feel less guilty."

Frances favoured her with a slightly withering glance. "You understand nothing, my obstinate child, so perhaps you'd better go on feeling guilty for a little longer. Really, Sarah, I've no patience with you! You have more intelligence and insight in your little finger than Sylvie has in her whole make-up, yet you choose to wear blinkers out of some idiotic sense of inferiority — all right, don't say it! I know your father and I have both been to blame — I more particularly because I hadn't his excuse for having failed to grow up — but I've always given you the credit for recognizing his blind spot with admirable tolerance. One forgets, I daresay, that at eighteen one is still vulnerable, however much one's sensibilities may have matured."

"There's no need to reproach yourself, Aunt Fran," Sarah said, warmed by the tacit suggestion of an adult friendship, but shy of accepting what might well have sprung out of an unguarded moment. "I've never resented Sylvie sharing my home, you know — she's filled a niche for Father which was quite beyond my scope. Of course I used to wish, when I was younger, that I could charm him and please his eye with the same ease, but I wasn't jealous. I would have embarrassed him terribly, you see, if I'd spilled out a lot of daughterly devotion which he couldn't possibly cope with."

Frances filled the last of the vases with careful concentration. She was both moved and humbled by Sarah's simple acceptance of her situation, but the habit of years was not easy to break and she felt unable to handle a fresh emotional situation with any skill.

"Yes, you're probably right," she said, then. "Well, you'll find there are greater compensations if you look for them."

"Will I?" Sarah sounded polite but not very interested. "Has Willie come back?"

"I don't know, but in any case Hattie will be keeping him out of your father's way until the upset's blown over. Now, run along, Sarah, or we'll both be late for lunch and that won't please your father. His cold is making him tetchy."

Sarah took the can, recognizing an air of relief in the brisk dismissal. She would have liked to ask further questions but, having learnt to guard her own reservations against importunate curiosity, she respected those of others. She averted her eyes from the settle in the hall which looked prim and unfriendly without the clutter of masculine impedimenta which Adam usually left there and hurried through to the kitchen, anxious for news of the dog.

"Have you got Willie out here?" she asked Hattie who was starting to dish up the vegetables, but the old servant shook her head.

"An't seen 'un. Like as not 'e's cadging a meal off Granny and in no hurry to come home."

"Granny Coker?"

"Why not? Didn't her take 'e in when 'e lost an eye that time? Like as not 'e went for shelter there if 'e was feared to come back on account of the fire."

"Yes, I suppose he might have. He's rather fond of Granny."

"Which shows 'is bad blood," Hattie retorted with her usual inability to resist a crack at Granny.

"Well, if he *is* there, she'll send him off in due course. She'll know I'd be worried," Sarah said, and Hattie gave her a shrewd glance.

"Not like you to be so sensible, I must say," she sniffed, slamming the oven door on a dish of freshly drained potatoes. "The times you've traipsed after that animal when there weren't no need would fill a book."

Sarah said nothing. She found it hard to explain, even to herself, a vague reluctance to set out on yet another unnecessary search unless the events of yesterday had tired her more than she realized, but when lunch was finished and there was still no sign of the dog she began to grow anxious. It would do no harm to walk as far as the Hollow, and if Willie was not there, then she must search the moor in good earnest. For all Adam's contention that the dog had as many lives as a cat one could never be sure, she thought. If Rowe and his threats no longer constituted a danger, the moor had other perils and a frightened animal was often a defenceless animal.

As she trudged the shoulder of moor below Rams Tor to join the familiar track to the Hollow she discovered

181

the cause of her reluctance. It was not the prospect of a tiring and possibly fruitless search which had deterred her but the necessity for revisiting a place which held painful memories. It seemed so long ago that she and Adam had thrown coins to the piskies, and Granny had told their fortunes, that it was hardly possible that he had been with them for such a short time ... hardly possible to have come to know and love a person so well that nothing would ever be quite so carefree again....

As she left Rams Tor behind her, however, and followed the old coffin track, now so overgrown from disuse that the stones which marked it were barely visible, something of the moor's old magic stirred in her blood again and her pace quickened. The wind had dropped to a light breeze and the changing colours were sharp and clear; little pockets of vapour still hung about in the hollows, a reminder of yesterday's weeping mists, but there was nothing to suggest tears in this brilliant afternoon and Sarah, though her heart might be sore, felt her spirits lift to the familiar call of loved and remembered places. She would miss Adam unbearably, she knew, and the hurt which she had dealt to his pride would nag at her for a very long while, but she knew, too, that in time the ache would grow less, that she might even forget him, except as the stranger who had briefly stolen away her heart, and that was the saddest thought of all.

As she rounded Chuff Tor to start on the downward path she saw that the Hollow was still blanketed in fog. She plunged into the mist, reminded of yesterday's alarming encounter as her skin grew clammy and strange objects loomed up and vanished again, and wished she still had the comforting assurance of Adam beside her, then as she reached the stony bottom, she stepped quite suddenly into clearness. The mist, by some freak of temperature or rock formation, hung just a few feet above her head, converting the Hollow into a strange and rather eerie chamber, and she looked about her, still a little shaken, but relieved to see that smoke was coming out of the caravan's chimney.

"Granny!" she shouted, running up the steps and hammering on the door, "it's me — Sarah — have you got Willie in there?" There was no sound from within and she began knocking and calling again. If Granny was in a bad mood she was quite capable of refusing to open the door, or then again she could be picking up sticks, or foraging for strange plants at the other end of the Hollow for her numerous potions, but whatever the reason, it was plain that no dog would have remained silent while someone battered on the door, and Willie would certainly have recognized her voice.

"I wouldn't batter any more, if I were you, the wood's pretty rotten," said a familiar and totally unexpected voice. "I must say, young woman, you've taken your time. I was nearly abandoning my vigil."

She stared up at Adam with her fists still raised and went so white that he made an instinctive movement towards her, then she bowed her face in her hands and, without warning, burst into tears. She stood on the bottom step of the caravan and wept as she had not wept for years, and he picked her up without more ado and brought her inside.

"Not very clean, I'm afraid, but you're used to Granny's squalor," he said as he propped her up on the narrow bunk and sat down beside her. "Now, my poor dear, cry it all out and don't mind me — didn't I tell you that one day I might be able to do you a good turn by unleashing those obstinate tears? So you can pay me the compliment of making use of my manly chest and having a good spring-clean."

She turned her face into his shoulder, only half taking in what he said, but neither surprise nor shame could interfere with the luxury of that moment. She wept in his arms with the uncaring abandon of a child, and had

183

no thought for anything but the comfort she found there.

"Well now," he said, when at last she was quieter and beginning to edge away, "that should clear the air for arriving at more sensible conclusions — no, don't try to get away from me and roll up again like your prototype the hedgehog — it's time we came to an understanding."

"I don't understand anything," she said. "Where's Granny?"

"Sitting in my car at the other end of the Hollow and probably well away with the flask of brandy I left as consolation. A pity about that — you could have done with a nip, as things have turned out."

"But I still don't understand. You'd left for Cornwall and — and I only came here after Willie, and he's n-not here."

"Willie is also sitting in my car, sharing a somewhat protracted vigil with Granny. I had some difficulty, I may say, in persuading your troublesome tyke to leave home again."

"You mean you deliberately *stole* Willie when he was home all the time?"

"Well, yes, I did. You can't blame me for practising a little low cunning when you clearly weren't going to come to terms, can you? You would have died sooner than ask me to stop on and finish my visit, wouldn't you, now?"

She was silent, remembering how she had regretted her lost opportunities, then said:

"Would it have made any difference?"

"I think so. At least we might have straightened out the hasty conclusions concerning those letters."

"The hasty conclusions were yours. You believed Sylvie's story."

"And you said nothing to disabuse me when given the chance."

"It hardly seemed worth while, besides—"

184

"Besides what?"

"You seemed to think I'd developed a — a schoolgirl crush for you, and that was highly distasteful to me."

"Was it, indeed? And do you suppose it wasn't any the less distasteful to me?" he retorted, then swore mildly as he observed her stricken face.

"Oh, my darling child, don't look like that!" he said quickly, trying to pull her back into his arms. "I only meant that the last thing I wanted was an adolescent infatuation. When a man well into his thirties falls in love he demands more than that to satisfy his needs, and I'd paid you the compliment long ago of appreciating that you weren't a child."

"Had you? Then you had a very odd way of treating me as a woman," she replied with something of her former tartness, and he grinned.

"But you, my dear, were so bent on fobbing me off with a display of prickles that I hadn't much option."

"Prackles," she murmured absently.

"Prackles — I stand corrected. Now, will you kindly stop interrupting and give me your attention. When will you marry me?"

She supposed it was the acrid fumes from the stove combined with the sour smell rising from Granny's blankets which suddenly made her feel light-headed and a little sick, but she made one last effort to preserve her dignity.

"Really, Professor! You don't have to go to such lengths to restore my self-respect," she said, and his mouth twitched.

"Really, Miss Hedgehog! And you don't have to throw my proposal back in my face with such airy unconcern," he retorted. "I can assure you my magnanimity doesn't stretch that far! Now you look me in the eye and say with truth that my offer repels you?" His hands cupped her face, forcing her to look at him, and although he had spoken so lightly, she saw a hint of

185

strain deepening the lines round his mouth and a questioning tenderness in his steady regard.

"How can you be sure? After Sylvie, how can you possibly be sure?" she asked him simply.

"Shall I show you?" Still cupping her face between his hands, he bent his head to hers and as she felt his lips seeking out every line and contour of her face and finally her mouth with growing urgency, she knew there was no further need for resistance.

"You little wretch ..." he said softly, much later ... "how dared you hold out on me right to the bitter end ... do you know you almost succeeded in convincing me that it *was* that natural male arrogance of which you unkindly accused me that was giving me ideas?"

"Well, that was one up to me, wasn't it?" she said a little smugly. "Anyway, you weren't so clever as you make out. You thought I'd fallen for Nick."

"A natural assumption, perhaps, since he was younger and much better looking. However, we won't go into that. I think we had better release both Granny and Willie from bondage now that we've settled our affairs — besides, our trysting place is getting a trifle smelly."

He had left the door open, but even so, the caravan had become unbearably stuffy and she was glad to make a move. As she got up she caught a glimpse of her face in Granny's fly-blown mirror, and grimaced ruefully.

"If you can fancy yourself in love when I'm looking like this, Adam, I shouldn't need any further convincing, should I? I told you that when I cry I do it with hideous results, and now you know," she said, and he kissed her again with lingering tenderness, tasting the salt of her tears on his lips.

"For me you will always have charm, no matter how plain you may look ... charm and the loveliest attri-

186

bute of all, the gift of a loving spirit," he said, and lifted her down from the caravan steps.

"Will you come back to Slattery now?" she asked as they made their way back to the car.

"I'll take you home, certainly, but as I will be leaving in a few days, anyhow, I think I'll stick to my present plans. That will give your charming cousin time to get her bearings — she's not going to be very pleased with either of us," he answered with a faint twinkle, and she stopped dead, looking thoroughly guilty.

"What on earth will Father say?" she exclaimed, remembering her family's hopes of Adam's intentions.

"I had the customary talk with your father before I left this morning. He was extremely affable and inclined to preen himself on his own perspicacity in having, so he says, guessed my little secret. You'll find your stock has risen considerably, so make the most of your new consequence," Adam replied rather dryly, tossing a pebble into the piskie pool, and Sarah looked shocked.

"That's tantamount to an insult," she told him reprovingly, temporarily diverted. "You'd better throw in some silver quickly or the piskies might take their revenge and put a curse on us."

"No," said Adam, taking her arm to march her firmly on, "I'm fully capable of looking after our interests without the dubious aid of the piskies, and I've pandered to Granny's crafty superstitions quite enough for one day."

"Adam," Sarah said when later on he drove her slowly up the hill through the blanketing mist and they emerged suddenly into sunlight, "will you stop here for a moment?" He pulled up at once on a strip of moorland. He slipped an arm round her shoulders, but he said nothing. He knew quite well that she wanted to shake off the nebulous unease of the Hollow, for he felt the same way himself, but as he watched her feasting her eyes on the wild, timeless spread of country, he thought, with a little pang, that she was already bidding farewell to the gods and dreams of her childhood.

"None of this need be lost to you," he said with gentleness. "Wherever our travels may take us, we will always come back ... you made me familiar with so much that you love in those letters, Sarah, and I want to share the magic with you — some had already rubbed off on me before ever I came to Slattery, you see."

"How understanding you are — how very understanding and dear ... that came through your letters, too, so no wonder I fell in love with a stranger.'"

"Did you, Sarah? But then, you see, we were never really strangers, you and I ... I must have loved the writer of those letters long before I guessed the truth."

Willie on the back seat feeling himself neglected for long enough, made a lunge forward, covering her neck and ears with sycophantic licks which never failed to command attention, but she absently pushed him away, to Adam's secret amusement.

"When did you guess?"

"I've no idea. Does it matter?"

"No."

She rested against his shoulder in great contentment, watching the scattered tors starting to cast their grotesque shadows over the moor. Up here the last of the sunlight still lingered, but down in the shadowed coombe, lights were beginning to spring up in cottage windows. It must be nearly tea-time, she thought, and said:

"Dear Professor ... dear, dear Professor ... how strange that I thought of you for so long as a Nose and a Beard."

"The conventional father-figure, no doubt, but don't let that fool you," he retorted. "I've no intention of adopting that role when I take to myself a wife, though I wouldn't mind switching occasionally to fill the gap, my poor starved hedgehog."

"What you've never had you don't miss, so they say, and if you go on calling me a hedgehog I shall divorce you," Sarah said with the old tartness, and he grinned.

"You can hardly do that till we're married, so give those prickles a rest," he replied, turning on the ignition.

"Prackles," she retaliated promptly, then succumbed to an unseemly fit of giggles as he fended off Willie who was attacking again from the rear, and swung the car back on to the road.

To our devoted Harlequin Readers:
Fill in handy coupon below and send off this page.

Harlequin Romances

TITLES STILL IN PRINT

51505 PAPER HALO, K. Norway

51506 THE FLOWERING CACTUS, I. Chace

51507 MARRIAGE BY REQUEST, L. Gillen

51508 CHILD OF MUSIC, M. Burchell

51509 A SUMMER TO REMEMBER, H. Pressley

51510 MAKE WAY FOR TOMORROW, G. Bevan

51511 WHERE BLACK SWANS FLY, D. Cork

51512 THAT MAN SIMON, A. Weale

51513 CHANGE OF DUTY, M. Norrell

51514 THE CASTLE OF THE SEVEN LILACS, V. Winspear

51515 O KISS ME, KATE, V. Thian

51516 THOSE ENDEARING YOUNG CHARMS, M. Malcolm

51517 CROWN OF FLOWERS, J. Dingwell

51518 THE LIGHT IN THE TOWER, J. S. Macleod

51519 SUMMER COMES TO ALBAROSA, I. Danbury

51520 INTO A GOLDEN LAND, E. Hoy

MAIL THIS COUPON TODAY

∞∞∞∞∞∞∞∞∞∞∞∞∞∞∞∞∞∞∞∞∞∞

Harlequin Books, Dept. Z

Simon & Schuster, Inc., 11 West 39th St.
New York, N.Y. 10018

☐ Please send me information about Harlequin Romance Sub-
scribers Club.

Send me titles checked above. I enclose .50 per copy plus .25
per book for postage and handling.

Name ....

Address ....

City .... State .... Zip ....